"Would you like to see something else?"
Roxy asked

Tom was ready to howl in frustration. "Yes, please."

Roxy backed away a bit so he would get the full effect, placed her hands on her thighs and began gathering the fabric of her skirt into her palms. The hem rose, inch by excruciating inch, revealing the tops of her bright red boots, the lacy white stockings...

"Aw, Slim!" he groaned. "Don't stop now."

"Remember the last time, when you tore my panties off?"

The skirt rose a half inch higher, revealing a slice of bare skin above the tops of the stockings.

He started to sweat. "Yes. I remember."

"Do you know why you won't have to rip my panties off?"

"No," he said, but he could guess.

"Because—" she lifted the skirt all the way up "—I'm not wearing any."

Blaze™

Dear Reader,

Like a lot of people, I have always been fascinated by the cowboy myth, and have long wanted to write a book set in the world of the rodeo. Now, those of you who are longtime romance fans may remember that I did do a sort of rodeo book once before, but the particular cowboy in that book (*Luck of the Draw*, Harlequin Temptation #608) was a *retired* bull rider and the rodeo merely provided the background for the story. This time I wanted my characters to be fully immersed in that special world.

To that end, I did loads of research (always one of my favorite parts of writing a book!). I watched movies about the rodeo and read books about it. I subscribed to *Prorodeo Sports News* and visited the Professional Rodeo Cowboy Association online (www.prorodeo.com/) to learn about the rules of the game. I went to rodeos. And, best of all, I interviewed cowboys. Lots of cowboys.

And so, taking bits and pieces of what I learned and tumbling them all around in my writer's imagination, thus was born Tom Steele, the quintessential rodeo cowboy, and the hero of this book.

It took a little longer to find my heroine. I needed just the right kind of woman to be able to stand up to that bigger-than-life cowboy myth. She had to be strong and sexy and sassy, with an attitude. It wasn't until I met a sixty-two-year-old retired barrel racer from San Antonio, who gave me some wonderful words of advice about rodeo cowboys, that the character of Roxy finally gelled for me.

I hope you enjoy Tom and Roxy's story. I certainly did.

Best wishes,

Candace Schuler

P.S. You can contact me through my Web site at www.CandaceSchuler.com. And check out www.tryblaze.com!

GOOD TIME GIRL

Candace Schuler

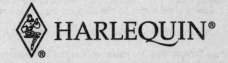

TORONTO • NEW YORK • LONDON
AMSTERDAM • PARIS • SYDNEY • HAMBURG
STOCKHOLM • ATHENS • TOKYO • MILAN • MADRID
PRAGUE • WARSAW • BUDAPEST • AUCKLAND

To all the good girls of the world who are yearning
to take a walk on the wild side—Go for it!

ISBN 0-373-79031-7

GOOD TIME GIRL

Visit us at www.eHarlequin.com

Printed in U.S.A.

Prologue

ROXANNE ARCHER designed her strategy like a four-star general—or a stalker.

The first part of the plan involved laying the groundwork. She studied her subject carefully. She plotted her itinerary. She listed her needs and requirements, defining and refining them as necessary. She carved out the time she would need. She saved the necessary funds. She acquired the necessary skills.

That had taken nearly six months to accomplish.

The second part of the plan involved general reconnaissance and one-on-one surveillance. She trailed several possible subjects, observing them in their natural habitat for several days before narrowing the field down to one. And then she trailed that one, learning his preferences, his habits, his predilections and inclinations.

That had taken nearly two weeks.

The third part was more hands-on. Bravely, she turned herself over to the experts and let them arm her for the coming campaign. She was plucked and waxed, trimmed and highlighted, buffed and filed and polished within an inch of her life. Then she selected and donned her camouflage so she would blend in with her surroundings.

That took nearly two days.

She was now as ready as she would ever be.

It was time to go get herself a good-looking, dangerous cowboy.

1

"WELL, I'M HERE to tell you, sugar, rodeo cowboys are a whole hell of a lot of fun but they're the most irresponsible sons o' bitches in the world when it comes to women. You can't trust 'em any farther than you can throw 'em, and you sure as hell can't believe a word they say. Especially the good-lookin' ones. They're the most dangerous kind, you know, 'cause they've been gettin' by on looks and charm their whole lives and they got it down to a science. I'm tellin' you the pure honest-to-God truth here, sugar. You got to keep an extra sharp eye on the good-lookin' ones or you'll get your poor little heart broke for sure."

Roxanne Archer heard those cautionary words of advice echo through her mind as she pulled into one of the few remaining parking spaces in front of Ed Earl's Polynesian Dance Palace, and resolutely reaffirmed her decision not to let the dire warnings of one crusty old ex-barrel racer from San Antonio put a damper on her quest.

She was going to get herself a cowboy.

A good-looking one.

The most dangerous kind.

If she got her heart broken in the process, well, so

be it. It was no more than she expected, in any case. And a broken heart had to be better than one that had shriveled up from disuse. Not to mention a few other body parts that were in imminent danger of dehydration from prolonged neglect.

She turned off the ignition of her rented candy-apple-red Mustang convertible and sat there for a moment, her fingers still clasping the key, her foot on the parking brake, staring blindly at the flock of pulsating pink-neon flamingos atop the roof of Ed Earl's, and contemplated the series of events—the series of *non*-events, actually—that had brought her to a cowboy honky-tonk on the outskirts of Lubbock, Texas, in the middle of her summer vacation. It was simple, really.

Roxanne Archer had been a good girl—a very good girl—for the entire twenty-nine, uneventful years of her life. She wanted to take a crack at being a good-time girl before it was too late. If it wasn't already too late. She'd been mired in good-girlness an awfully long time, and it was an awfully deep rut to climb out of—even with the help of a dangerous, good-looking cowboy.

Provided, of course, that she actually managed to get herself one.

"I just won't go home *until* I get him," she muttered stubbornly, and reached up to flip open the lighted makeup mirror in the visor so she could check her lipstick—glossy candy-apple red like the car—and make sure her hair hadn't blown all to pieces on her drive over from the Broken Spoke Motel. It had. But as promised by the young woman who'd cut it for her in Dallas just two days ago, being blown all to pieces had only improved the style. Roxanne smiled at herself, delighted by the chunky, layered cut that tangled with her eyelashes and caressed the back of her neck with such reckless abandon.

It was amazing what a new hairdo could do for a woman. Not to mention a new shade of lipstick. And new clothes. Especially when each and every item of those new clothes—right down to the leopard-print bikini panties and matching push-up demi bra—were so radically different from what said woman usually wore.

Feeling wild and wicked and blessedly unlike her usual boring self, Roxanne pushed the car door open, swung her feet out onto the graveled parking lot, straightened up to her full five feet nine inches...and teetered precariously as the high, stacked heels of her brand-new, lipstick-red Sweetheart of the Rodeo cowboy boots sank into the rocky, uneven surface. She made a hasty grab for the top of the car door to steady herself, wondering if maybe the high-heeled boots had been a mistake. She always wore flats at home, or sensible pumps with little one-inch heels so she didn't tower over people—men—any more than necessary.

But, then, no, she told herself firmly, good-time girls didn't wear sensible shoes, whether they towered over people or not.

And, besides, she'd always wanted a pair of red cowboy boots, ever since she was a little girl growing up in Greenwich, Connecticut, secretly dreaming about riding the range as a dangerous outlaw queen like Belle Starr or Cat Ballou. Although it didn't actually say so in any of the books she'd read, she'd been absolutely positive an outlaw queen would wear red cowboy boots. She'd gathered up her courage and asked her mother for a pair.

Charlotte Hayworth Archer had lectured her nine-year-old daughter about her poor choice of role models and footwear, then bought her proper brown leather riding boots and a proper English saddle and signed her up for proper riding lessons, no doubt believing all that wholesome, healthful propriety would rechannel Roxanne's interests and ambitions in a more socially acceptable direction.

Which it had.

Sort of.

Roxanne learned to keep her admiration for unconventional women to herself, and she never mentioned her desire for red boots again.

After a while, she *almost* forgot she'd ever wanted them. Dressage riders didn't wear fancy red boots, nor did honor students or members of the debate team or the Latin club, and certainly no class valedictorian had ever pranced across the stage to the podium in red boots. A cheerleader might, of course, or a member of the drama club, but Roxanne was too tall and too inhibited and…well, just too plain geeky to belong to either of those cliques. A girl like Roxanne had been during her high school years—tall, gangly, scholarly, shy—would never wear or do or say anything to attract attention to herself. It got to be a habit, and Roxanne passed out of her awkward teens and into her marginally less awkward twenties without attracting any undue notice from anyone.

Shortly after her twenty-fourth birthday she became one half of a mature adult relationship with another teacher at the exclusive private school were she taught English Lit and beginning Latin to fifth graders, but she never really attracted his attention, either. Not completely. In the three years they spent together as a couple, he never once remembered how she liked her coffee—a *half* a spoonful of sugar, damn it!—or noticed that she faked her orgasms.

Which, in a roundabout way, was the reason she was standing in front of a cowboy honky-tonk outside of Lubbock, Texas, in the middle of her summer vacation, wearing red cowboy boots and the shortest, tightest skirt she'd ever worn in her life.

Roxanne Archer was finally ready to call some attention to herself, to cut loose, to kick over the traces, to take a walk on the wild side and find out what all the shouting was about. In the immortal words of Auntie Mame—another admirably unconventional woman with a flamboyant fashion sense—Roxanne was ready to "live, live, live!"

For the duration of her vacation, anyway.

She let go of the car door, then reached down with both hands—freshly manicured with glossy fire-engine-red polish instead of her usual tasteful French manicure—and carefully smoothed her sweaty palms over the curve of her hips to make sure her tiny denim skirt was still covering everything it was supposed to cover.

Someone whistled appreciatively

Roxanne started at the unexpected sound, her body stiffening instinctively, as if to ward off a threat or an insult. And then, deliberately, remembering her mission, she forced herself to relax. She'd dressed to attract attention, hadn't she? Well, she'd attracted attention. Now she just had to figure out what to do with it.

She turned her head slightly, glancing over her shoulder, and flashed what she hoped was a saucy smile at her admirer.

The response was immediate. And immensely gratifying.

He puffed up like a rooster and swaggered toward her with the loose-limbed, bow-legged gait of a man who'd spent a lot of time on a horse. "Well, hey, there, baby doll," he crooned appreciatively as he honed in on her.

He was six foot four, at least, with shoulders like a bull, a trophy buckle the size of a pancake decorating his belt, and a smile as wide and open as a Texas prairie beaming out at her from under the rim of a cream-colored Stetson. An honest-to-goodness cowboy. Good-looking, too, in an open, aw-shucks, country boy sort of way that, unfortunately, wasn't the least bit dangerous.

Roxanne had her heart firmly set on dangerous.

Still, a cowboy was a cowboy, even if he had freckles and a snub nose. And she could certainly use the practice. She fluttered her eyelashes experimentally.

"Hey, yourself, sugar," she drawled. Her accent was a near perfect imitation of the San Antonio barrel racer who had warned her against trusting cowboys. The flirtatious tilt of her head was the result of two weeks' worth of close observation and diligent practice in front of a mirror. Amazingly, it worked.

The cowboy swaggered a bit closer and leaned in, putting one big, beefy hand on the open car door. The mingled scents of horses, saddle soap and a musky men's cologne, liberally applied, engulfed her. "You here alone, baby doll?"

Roxanne stifled the urge to take a quick step backward, out of range of that too strong cologne and the unfamiliar burden of his undivided attention. It was what she would have done. Before. Now, she shut the car door with a sassy little thrust of her hip, dislodging his hand, and gave him what she hoped was a provocative look from under the fringe of her chunky blond bangs. "I'm meeting someone inside."

"Girlfriend?" he said, looking so much like an eager, oversize puppy that Roxanne couldn't help but smile at him again.

"Boyfriend." She touched the manicured tip of her index finger to the center of his massive chest and pushed lightly, backing him up. "And he's real jealous, sugar, so I'd be careful if I were you."

The cowboy's grin widened. "I'm willing to take a chance if you are, baby doll. We could run away together before he even knows you're here. My truck's right over there."

Roxanne laughed and shook her head, causing her tousled flyaway cut to shimmer in the pink neon glow of the flock of flamingos gracing the roof of Ed Earl's. "I wouldn't want your death on my conscience, sugar. But thanks for the invitation." She sighed regretfully. "It was a real sweet offer and if I wasn't otherwise engaged, I'd be tempted." She batted her eyelashes again for good measure. "I really would."

She patted his chest and turned away, tucking the car key into the pocket of her stretch denim skirt as she sauntered across the parking lot—slowly, because of the unaccustomed height of her boot heels and the graveled surface beneath her feet. The careful pace made her hips sway seductively, in a way they never did in her usual flats.

"Man, oh, man," she heard him say reverently, and she slowed down even more, exaggerating the fluid movement of her hips, enjoying the moment, reveling in her unexpected success.

Oh, it had been so easy! Who would have ever believed it would be so easy?

With a triumphant, self-satisfied smile tugging at the corners of her glossy red lips, Roxanne pulled open the front door of Ed Earl's Polynesian Dance Palace and sashayed in like she owned the place.

It was as if she had stepped into another world and—like Dorothy torn from her black-and-white life and thrust over the rainbow into a brilliantly colored Oz—she could only stand there and blink in stupefied amazement. It was loud, smoky, and tacky. Unapologetically, unrepentantly, *gloriously* tacky.

Chinese paper lanterns were strung from life-size wooden cutouts shaped like palm trees. Brightly colored plastic fish dangled from the ceiling. Bedraggled fisherman's netting, studded with glass floats, striped beach balls and pink plastic flamingos of various sizes, was draped across the walls. Gyrating hula dolls—the kind found on the dashboards of cars of people with questionable taste—decorated each table. The wait staff wore gaudy Hawaiian Aloha shirts and paper flower leis with their Wranglers and boots. The four members of the twanging cowboy band stood on a small, raised stage constructed to look like a log raft. The crowded dance floor was huge, kidney-shaped and painted a vivid blue. Roxanne's cocky smile faltered a bit as she watched the dancers' whirling, skipping, kicking progress around the scuffed blue floor.

Dancing had never been her strong suit. Not that she didn't love to dance. She did. But girls who were five feet nine inches tall by the time they were thirteen, especially girls who were brainy and wore glasses, too, didn't get much opportunity to learn all the latest dance moves. Her mother had insisted she learn all the standard ballroom dances, of course— and what a wretched embarrassment those lessons had been, being waltzed around the room by an unwilling partner whose head barely reached her chin!—but she'd never danced any of the popular dances all the kids her age were doing back in high school. Not in public, anyway.

Determined not to be left out this time around, she'd secretly taken a six-week series of dance lessons in preparation for her Wild West adventure, but none of the half a dozen country-western dances she'd so painstakingly learned bore more than a passing resemblance to the bewildering series of steps currently being performed on the floor of Ed Earl's Polynesian Dance Palace. Obviously, her instructors—a fresh-faced young preppie couple in matching pastel plaid shirts—had never been in a Texas honky-tonk. Or six weeks of lessons hadn't been nearly enough. Either way, she couldn't possibly—

"Dance, ma'am?"

Roxanne shifted her gaze from the dance floor to find another cowboy smiling at her from beneath the rim of a broad-brimmed, black cowboy hat. This one was lean and rangy, with dark, soulful eyes and an uncanny resemblance to a young John Travolta. Unfortunately, he was also no more than twenty, at most. Still, it was heartening to be hit on as soon as she came in the door, as it were. Another sign, if she needed one, that her transformation from party pooper to party girl had been successful. If she hadn't been ninety-nine percent sure she'd fall flat on her face, she might have taken him up on his offer, just out of pure gratitude that he'd asked.

"Thank you, no." She smiled at him to cushion the blow. "I'm meeting someone." She gestured across the sea of dancers toward the bar and pool tables on the other side of the blue lagoon. "Over there."

"How 'bout I dance you over that way, then? Little bitty slip of a thing like you might get stomped on, you try to make it through this rowdy crowd on your own."

Even without the warning from the San Antonio barrel racer about a rodeo cowboy's proclivity for stretching the truth, Roxanne knew a line when she heard one—and his was long enough to hang clothes on. No one had ever, in all her twenty-nine years, referred to her as a "little bitty slip of a thing." She'd been called skinny. Scrawny. Bean Pole. String Bean. Arrow Archer. But *never* a little bitty slip of a thing.

And by someone who was smiling at her as if he really, truly meant it. At the moment, anyway. It was irresistible.

"All right, sugar," she drawled, suddenly feeling powerfully, erotically female. *Little bitty slip of a thing.* If she could call forth that kind of shameless flattery from a young, good-looking cowboy by just standing there, she could do anything. Even dance in public without disgracing herself. "For that, you get one dance. The man I'm meeting can wait."

He whooped as if he'd just won the lottery and snagged an arm around her waist, whirling her onto the floor before she had a chance to change her mind.

"One dance," she reiterated as they joined the enthusiastic throng.

They danced two dances.

After all, the first dance hardly counted, as the song was more than half over when they joined in. And the second dance was the Cotton-Eyed Joe. It would be an affront to Texans everywhere to leave the dance floor when the Cotton-Eyed Joe was playing. Roxanne acquiesced to that argument, spurious though it was, but managed to stand firm when he tried to cajole her into a third go-round. Cute as he was—and he was darn cute!—she had other plans for the evening. And it was about time she quit stalling and put them into action.

"I'm meeting someone," she stated firmly, resisting when her dance partner tried to twirl her into the two-step that was just beginning. "And you said you'd dance me over there—" she gestured with her free hand "—after *one* dance, now didn't you, sugar?"

The cowboy gave an exaggerated shrug, pantomiming both compliance and disappointment, and obligingly two-stepped her backward through the crowd. As they approached the edge of the dance floor, he spun her in a series of quick, showy turns that ended with her pressed up against his lean, rock-hard young body, their joined hands clasped against the small of her back. Breathless, laughing, Roxanne clutched at his shoulder with her free hand for balance and found herself looking into his face from only inches away. The expression in his soulful brown eyes had her reconsidering her definition of dangerous.

"Oh, my." She slid her hand from his shoulder to his chest in an effort to give herself a little more breathing room. Unlike the cowboy who'd accosted her in the parking lot, he didn't budge. "Well…um, that was certainly invigorating," she said brightly, forgetting to drawl. "Thank you."

"Thank *you*," he purred, and dipped his head with unmistakable intent.

Roxanne drew back sharply, as far as the arm encircling her waist would permit.

"Is that a no?" he murmured.

"No. I mean, yes. That's a no," she stammered, fighting a curious combination of schoolgirl panic and equally schoolgirlish triumph.

He wanted to kiss her!

It was out of the question, of course. He was just a kid. Younger than her youngest brother, Edward, who was a junior at Brown. But still…this young John

Travolta lookalike wanted to kiss *her!* It was a heady thought and if he were a few years older or she were a few years younger, she might be tempted to let him. Maybe.

"Sure I can't change your mind? I know lots of other—" his arm tightened fractionally, pressing her closer to his overheated body; his voice dropped an octave, becoming intimate and suggestive "—invigoratin' things we can do together."

"Yes, I'm quite sure you do," she said primly, wondering how she'd gotten herself into this. And how she was going to get out of it. "But I'm meet—" She sucked in her breath, startled into silence when he reached up and brushed her cheek with the back of one finger.

"You sure have soft skin," he murmured, his finger wandering down her cheek to the side of her neck. His dark eyes sizzled with potent male heat. "You this soft all over?"

Roxanne reached up and grabbed his hand, stopping its unerring descent toward the scooped neckline of her lace-edged camisole blouse. "No," she said firmly, with no equivocation in her voice this time, and no indecision in her expression that might lead him to think she could be convinced to change her mind.

The young cowboy sighed and let her go. "I enjoyed the dance. Dances," he said with a smile, as earnest and polite as if he hadn't just tried to cop a feel. "And if you change your mind about anything—" his voice took on a playful, suggestive timbre "—you just give a holler and I'll come runnin'."

His easy, good-natured capitulation to her rejection boosted Roxanne's confidence another notch. Obviously, she was better at this man/woman thing than she'd thought. Or, rather, her sexy alter ego was better at it.

"And just who should I holler for, sugar?" She tilted her head, looking up at him from beneath her lashes. "If I do happen to change my mind, that is."

"The name's Clay." He offered his hand. "Clay Madison."

Roxanne put hers into it. "Roxy Archer," she said, giving him the version of her name she'd decided went with her new persona.

"Well, Roxy, it's been a real pleasure." He lifted the hand he held to his lips and brushed a careless kiss across her knuckles before letting it go. "You remember what I said now, hear? Holler if you change your mind."

"I'll do that," she promised mendaciously, knowing it wouldn't happen.

Clay Madison knew it, too. He touched two fingers to the brim of his hat in a brief cowboy salute, then turned and left her standing at the edge of the dance floor while he zeroed in on a big-haired, big-bosomed young lovely in skintight jeans and a skinny little tank top that exposed a great deal more cleavage than Roxanne could ever hope to possess, even with the help of a push-up bra.

"Oh, well," she said to herself, watching without rancor as he twirled the delighted girl onto the crowded dance floor with the same smooth moves he'd used on her. "Easy come, easy go."

She had no doubt at all that if she'd been willing, it could have been her out on the dance floor, plastered up against young Clay Madison with his hand inching inexorably toward her butt. It was a comforting thought. Before Clay and the cowboy in the parking lot, her belief in her ability to inspire that kind of lustful feeling in a man had been based on little more than research and hope. Now, it was established fact. She could do it. She *had* done it. She could do it again. All it took, apparently, was a short, tight skirt, a provocative smile, and the ability to flutter her eyelashes.

She was utterly amazed it had taken her nearly twenty-nine years to figure out something so simple, but now that she had, she was going to put her new knowledge to good use. With a confident toss of her head, Roxanne turned and headed for the bar with a sultry, hip-swinging stride that drew more than one admiring male glance.

"Lone Star," she purred when the bartender smiled and asked her pleasure.

She waved away the mug he brought with the beer, wrapped her hand around the frosty long-necked bottle and swiveled around on her bar stool so she was facing the pool table tucked into the far corner of the honky-tonk. She raised the beer to her lips and took a long, slow swallow, surveying the men playing pool over the upturned end of the bottle.

There he was.

Her cowboy.

The good-looking, dangerous one.

She lowered the beer, resting the cool frosty bottom

on her bare knee, and watched him as he circled the
pool table with the cue in his hand. He wasn't movie-
star handsome like young Clay Madison, but Roxanne
didn't want movie-star handsome. She wanted craggy
and rugged. She wanted virile and manly. A real cowboy, not the rhinestone version.

The cowboy playing pool was as real as it got.

He was long and lean, an even six feet according
to his stats, although his boots and hat made him seem
taller. Broad at the shoulders and narrow at the hips
with the strong, hard thighs of a horseman, he moved
around the pool table with the ambling, easy, loose-
kneed gait of a man who knew the value of patience.
He was older than most of the other rodeo cowboys—
an important consideration to a woman staring her
thirtieth birthday in the face—with tiny lines of experience etched into the tanned skin around his eyes,
and laugh lines creasing his lean cheeks. His dark hair
was conservatively cut, neither short nor long, with
the appealing tendency to curl from underneath the
edges of his hat. His snap-front, Western-cut shirt was
a plain, pale blue; his jeans were snug but not tight;
the silver trophy buckle on his belt was moderately
sized. His whole manner bespoke quiet, rock-solid
confidence with no need to advertise either his phy-
sique or his prowess.

Roxanne had been surreptitiously watching him for
the past two weeks, sizing him up from the safety of
the stands and around the rodeo grounds. Now, her
decision made, her quarry in sight, she leveled her
gaze at him from across the room and stared openly,
her interest obvious to anyone who cared to look.

The object of her interest stood, hip cocked, head down, the brim of his hat shadowing his face, his upper body bent over the pool table as he lined up his shot, seemingly oblivious to the woman watching him.

Roxanne kept staring, willing him to look up. According to all the books she'd read and the research she'd done in preparation for her Wild West adventure, the easiest and most direct way for a woman to signal her interest in a man was with eye contact. Prolonged, direct eye contact. The trick, she realized now, was to get him to look at her in the first place. The books and magazine articles had made it all sound so simple. Catch his eye, lick your lips, trail your fingertips suggestively over your cleavage or the rim of your glass, all the while holding that all important eye contact, and he'd come running. That was the theory, anyway. Unfortunately, nothing she'd read had mentioned what to do if he was so intent on his next pool shot that he didn't even notice you were staring at him.

She was just about to switch tactics, steeling herself to slide off the bar stool and saunter over to the pool table for a more direct approach when, suddenly, his shoulders twitched under the pale blue fabric of his shirt. His hands stilled on the pool cue. He raised his head, slowly, his upper body still positioned over the felt-covered table in preparation for his shot.

She saw the chiseled angle of his jaw first as it emerged from beneath the shadow of his hat…the full, sculpted curve of his lips…his blade of a nose…the strong, angled cheekbones under skin the warm golden color of old doubloons…and then, finally, the startling blue of his eyes as he looked straight at her from under the brim of his hat.

Their gazes locked.

Held.

Roxanne felt the jolt all the way down to her toes. *Steady,* she told herself, fighting the urge to lower her gaze. *Steady.* Now wasn't the time to get all girlie and flustered. She'd caught his attention. Now she had to engage his interest enough to make him approach her. Deliberately, with a gesture she'd practiced a hundred times in front of the mirror in preparation for this moment, she lifted her free hand and touched her crimson-tipped fingers to the lace-trimmed edge of her scoop-necked blouse, brushing them lightly, languidly, back and forth over the cleavage produced by the push-up bra.

The cowboy's eyes widened and his gaze flickered downward, following the sultry movement of her fingers on her skin. The expression in his blue eyes when they came back to hers was hot, focused and intent, rife with speculation and frank sexual curiosity.

Roxanne felt equal parts fear, excitement and sheer female power sizzling through her at the success of her ploy. She'd done it. She'd hooked him. Now all she had to do was reel him in.

Come to mama, she thought, and smiled in blatant, unmistakable invitation.

2

IT TOOK TOM STEELE a good ten seconds to convince himself the hot little blonde at the bar was actually aiming her come-hither stare at him. Not that he hadn't been the focus of a come-hither stare before. He did all right with the ladies. Always had. But the trophy-hunting buckle bunnies who hung out in places like Ed Earl's usually went after bigger trophies—and younger, flashier studs. There was nothing flashy about Tom Steele.

His last birthday had put him on the far side of thirty, for one thing, making him a good five to ten years older than most of the peach-fuzz cowboys in the honky-tonk. And even in his younger days he'd never been one of those Fancy Dans who went in for wildly colored custom-made shirts, glittery bat-wing chaps or oversize silver belt buckles. He was a circuit cowboy, and proud of it. A weekend competitor who fit his rodeoing in around a job and a ranch and an eighty-hour workweek.

Or rather, he *had* been a circuit cowboy.

This year—his last year before he quit for good—he'd decided to go hog wild and really live it up, competing in as many rodeos as possible, traveling from one go-round to the next, living, eating and breathing the foot loose and fancy free life of the professional rodeo cowboy for one full season. So far, that meant he spent a good deal of his time behind the wheel of his pickup, chasing the rodeo from one dusty Podunk town to another, living on fast food and bad coffee, and getting tossed around by snortin' mad broncs on a daily basis instead of just on the weekends.

It was a good life, as far as it went. The days were mostly hot and dirty, comprised of long periods of boredom and inactivity interspersed with eight-second intervals of heart-pounding, teeth-rattling, bone-jarring excitement. The nights were mostly spent on the road or in honky-tonks like Ed Earl's. He had no responsibilities to speak of beyond making sure he was paid up and on time for each of his events. And no worries beyond wondering which bronc he was going to draw in the next go-round. About the only thing missing from his last fling was, well…a last fling.

It appeared things might be looking up in that department.

"Well, hell, Tom. You gonna stand there, starin' at that little gal like some big dumb critter what ain't got no sense, or you gonna take your shot?"

Without shifting his gaze away from the woman at the bar, Tom straightened and handed his pool cue to the cowboy who'd asked the question. "I'm going to take my shot," he said.

"Hey, you got a twenty ridin' on this game," the cowboy reminded him.

Tom didn't even glance at the crumpled bills under

the shot glass on the edge of the pool table. "Consider it forfeit," he said. "I think I've just found a more interesting game to play." Then, paying no attention to the hoots and hollers that followed his comment, he rounded the end of the felt-covered table and headed toward the blonde at the bar.

He moved slowly, purposefully, the way he did when he was approaching the chute to climb aboard his next ride. His gait was measured and even, his boot heels clicking against the floor with every deliberate step, neither his gaze nor his pace wavering as he unerringly honed in on her through the noise and smoke of the jam-packed honky-tonk. She didn't fidget, didn't look away, didn't blush or giggle or toss her hair. She simply sat there, perched on the bar stool as regal as a princess—her back ramrod-straight, her long slim legs crossed at the knee, her hand playing idly at her breast—and watched him come to her.

She was a tall, cool glass of water, for sure, a far cry from the usual oversprayed, overdone, overeager groupies who congregated around rodeo cowboys. Long and lean with a glossy, high-tone polish, she had a pampered, well-bred look to her underneath the fancy packaging, like a Thoroughbred racehorse all decked out in a show pony rig. And, hot damn, what a rig!

Her short blond hair was kind of rumpled and tousled-looking, as if she'd just rolled out of bed and wouldn't mind rolling back in. Her lips were red and shiny, as if she'd just licked them. The tiny little skirt she was wearing showed off miles of slender, well-toned leg and clung like denim-colored Saran wrap to

the sweetest curve of hip it had ever been his privilege
to see. The neckline of her white blouse dipped just
low enough to offer a tantalizing glimpse of cleavage.
And those long, red nails…

Damn, she knew just what she was doing, brushing
those glossy red fingernails back and forth above the
scooped neckline of her blouse, all nonchalant and
casual-like, as if she had no idea she was doing it or
what the sight did to a man, with that mysterious,
knowing little smile curving those matching red lips,
offering compliance and challenge without a word being spoken. And all the while staring at him as if she
meant to gobble him up when he got close enough.

It riveted a man's attention, for sure, and got the
blood pumping through his veins harder than it did
when he was in the chute, sitting on top of twelve-
hundred pounds of quivering horseflesh and waiting
for the gate to swing open.

Tom did what he always did in that situation. He
narrowed his focus to the task at hand, settled in, and
prepared to take hold, determined to assert his domi-
nance from the get-go. Women or horses, he'd always
figured the game plan was pretty much the same. A
man had to show 'em who was boss, right off, or he'd
end up getting stomped on. Especially with the high-
spirited ones. And he could tell at a glance the long-
legged blonde with the cool, glossy polish and the hot
come-hither look in her eyes was definitely one of the
high-spirited ones. If a man let a woman like that get
the upper hand, he'd never get it back.

He came to a stop directly in front of her.

And then he just stood there, his jeans-clad knees

inches from her bare dimpled ones, his wide shoulders blocking her view of everything except him, and silently offered up a hot-eyed challenge of his own.

Her sassy little smile faltered a bit and the tip of her tongue came out, licking nervously at her bottom lip, but her gaze never wavered. "Buy you a drink, cowboy?" she purred.

Her voice was low and husky with a hint of something foreign and exotic under the drawl, as if she were from someplace other than Texas. Tom liked exotic, especially when it was sleek and blond and brazen. He pushed the brim of his hat up a fraction of an inch with the tip of his thumb, then, still silent, leaned in and put his hand on the bar beside her.

She shrank back, just slightly, and her gaze dropped for a split second. Then her spine stiffened and her chin came up, and she met his eyes. Five long seconds passed in silence as they stared at each other, deep blue eyes gazing into pale golden brown, male to female, yin to yang, speculation, curiosity and pure undisguised sexual energy crackling back and forth between them like static electricity as they silently jockeyed for position in the age-old battle of the sexes.

Then one of her eyebrows rose, all hoity-toity and imperious. "Well?" she said, and there was a snap under the cornpone and molasses in her voice. "Do you want a drink or not, sugar?"

Tom bit back a grin—damn, he liked a woman with sass!—and put his other hand on the bar, caging her between his outstretched arms. "How 'bout we skip the preliminaries, Slim,'' he said, his voice low and husky and suggestive, ''and just get right to it.''

Her eyes flared wide for a second, and he would have sworn he saw her gulp, but the angle of her chin stayed the same. ''Skip the preliminaries?''

He leaned in just a bit closer, all but surrounding her with his size and strength in a deliberate attempt to overwhelm her with the none-too-subtle body language of the dominant male animal. The grin he couldn't quite control curved his lips, quirking up one corner of his mouth when she refused to give ground by shrinking back a second time.

''No sense wasting time when we both know what we want, now is there?'' he said silkily, close enough now so that his knees were bumping hers and the brim of his hat shadowed her upturned face.

Roxanne lifted her free hand in automatic reflex, putting it against his chest in an instinctive effort to preserve what little space she had left, and opened her mouth to inform him in no uncertain terms that she wasn't that kind of girl. Fortunately, she remembered in time that she was, for the duration of her vacation, anyway, *exactly* that kind of girl. The problem was, she had no idea what that kind of girl would do now, with six gorgeous, well-muscled feet of cowboy all but pressing her up against the bar.

''Well...um....'' She stared up at him, her head tilted back, her hand resting lightly against his broad chest, her mind working frantically.

He was so close she could feel the warmth of his breath on her cheek, so close she could feel the brush of his shirtsleeves against her bare arms. The look in his deep blue eyes was confident and cocksure, as tempting as sin on a hot Saturday night. The heat of his body was an almost tangible thing, reaching out to curl around her like the loop of an expertly thrown lasso.

Her heartbeat quickened in response, sending an answering heat surging through her, making her nerve endings sizzle with a heady combination of panic and excitement as she tried to decide what her next move should be.

None of her carefully orchestrated plans for her fall from grace had included the possibility of falling quite so fast—and without any of the preliminaries he seemed so eager to dispense with. She'd expected at least a few minutes of getting-to-know-you pleasantries over that drink she'd intended to buy him. Maybe a dance or two to warm things up and put them both at ease. A little sweet talk and romantic nonsense to disguise what was really going on. Apparently, her good-looking, dangerous cowboy didn't believe in wasting time with subterfuge or romantic nonsense.

So, how would a real good-time girl handle the situation?

Hold him off?

Or urge him on?

Tom stood stock-still, waiting, his hands on the bar on either side of her, the little half smile still turning up one corner of his mouth, an unholy gleam of masculine devilry and undisguised anticipation lighting his face, and watched the whirl of emotions parade through her big whiskey-colored eyes as she debated the issue with herself.

He knew he'd disconcerted her with his direct-
ness—that had been his intent, after all—and he had
read, quite clearly, the first flash of instinctive, feminine outrage at his masculine arrogance and presumption. He also saw the flicker of uncertainty that replaced it, the swift calculation and consideration, the
bubbling excitement beneath it all that got his own
juices flowing fast and hot…and, then, suddenly, surprisingly, the unmistakable glint of steely-eyed resolve.

Tom bit back a curse and prepared to be slapped
down—verbally, at least—for daring to presume too
much, too soon. Any man with good sense knew the
high-spirited ones, be they equine or human, didn't
take kindly to being rushed. And no woman, high-
spirited or not, reacted favorably to the assumption
that she could be too easily had. Even when she could
be.

"You're absolutely right," she said briskly, surprising him again just as he was about to pull back
and regroup by asking her to dance—and pretending
that's what he'd meant all along.

"Ma'am?" he murmured vaguely, stalling for time
while he tried to figure out what he'd been right about.

"No sense wasting time when we both know what
we want." She turned slightly and set the bottle of
beer on the bar behind her with a decisive little click.
"Let's get to it," she said, and slid off the bar stool
into his wide-open arms.

Tom reacted automatically, shifting his weight
backward, lowering his hands from the edge of the
bar to catch her as she all but fell into his embrace.

He bracketed her hips in his wide palms, holding her upright, meaning only to steady her until she found her balance before he let her go again. But she was a warm, fragrant armful of woman, sleek and sexy and soft.

Incredibly soft.

Everywhere.

Her hair was soft against his jaw.

Her breath was soft against his neck.

Her breasts were soft against his chest.

And he was suddenly, incredibly, excruciatingly hard.

Everywhere.

The unexpectedness of it caught him completely off guard. The intensity of it short-circuited his brain, urging him to bypass the teasing, testing first steps of the mating dance they'd been doing in favor of the pure, primal male instinct to dominate and possess a willing female. Between one breath and the next, he forgot he'd been going to ask her to dance, forgot they'd only just met, forgot he didn't even know her name. Instinctively, without conscious thought or premeditation, he tightened his hands on the curve of her hips, pulling her solidly against his suddenly aching erection.

Roxanne gasped and her eyes widened, the pupils dilating until they all but obscured the golden brown of her irises. But she didn't stiffen. She didn't pull back. She didn't move by so much as a fraction of an inch. And she didn't look away.

Couldn't look away.

They stood there in the noisy honky-tonk in front

of the long, busy bar, chest to breast, belly to belly, groin to groin, and stared at each other as if they were the only two people in the place. The heat sizzling between them built exponentially, second by second, growing higher and hotter and more intense, until it was zigzagging back and forth like lightning on a stormy summer night. No words were spoken. None were needed.

He wanted her.

She wanted him.

It was as simple, as basic, as elemental as that.

Obeying rampant male instinct and the hot female invitation in her eyes, he bent his head and kissed her. One hard, ravening, devouring kiss, unmistakable in its carnality and erotic intent, as intimate and intemperate as if they were alone in a quiet bedroom. She kissed him back the same way, deeply, avidly, instinctively, her mouth open, her tongue tangling wildly with his for a long, hot, mindless moment out of time. And then they drew apart a fraction of an inch, both of them flushed, both of them breathing too fast, and stared at each other for another long moment. His hands were hot and hard on her hips, holding her securely against him. Hers were curled around his biceps, her shiny red nails pressing into the unyielding muscle beneath his pale blue shirt. Questions were asked and answered, decisions made as they stood there, silently staring into each other's eyes.

"Are you sure?" he growled, low, just to make certain he was reading her right.

"Yes," she murmured breathlessly, and then, more

firmly, "Yes, I'm sure," she said, and nodded her head for added emphasis.

Incredible as it seemed, she'd never been more sure of anything in her entire life. There wasn't a shred of doubt in her mind. Not a smidgen of hesitation. Not a second thought to be had. The earlier niggling fragment of panic had receded into absolute nothingness, wholly replaced by reckless excitement and wild anticipation for what was to come. She'd been waiting for this moment, fantasizing about it, her whole life. She wasn't about to chicken out now that the fantasy was within her grasp.

"Yes." The word was an affirmation—and a vow.

"You'll leave with me now?" he said, giving her another chance to come to her senses. "Just walk out of this bar with me right now? This minute?" His gaze was still inexorably locked with hers. His erection was unmistakable, pressed firmly against her pubic mound. His fingers bit into her hips. "Even knowing we're going to end up naked and sweaty ten minutes after you do?"

She nodded again. "Yes," she said, her tone unequivocal and rock-steady, despite the erratic fluttering of her heart and the rush of heat that flooded her body at his words and the feel of him against her.

"Then let's get the hell out of— Damn!" The word was a hot expulsion of air against her lips. "I don't have a room. I was planning on hitting the road later tonight so I didn't book a room."

And all the nearby hotels and motels would already be chock-full of the cowboys who *weren't* hitting the road until the next morning.

"Damn," he said again, his brows drawing together as he struggled to think through the thick cloud of lust in his brain and come up with an alternate plan.

There was always the front seat of his truck, but that didn't seem quite gentlemanly. And, besides, the way he was feeling, he was going to need a lot more than the front seat of a pickup to maneuver in, even if it was the biggest damn model Chevy made. Maybe he could work a trade with one of his buddies, or offer a little monetary incentive to someone to give up their room or... Hell, if there were absolutely no other accommodations to be had—and he was pretty sure there weren't—he was hot enough to forget his gentlemanly scruples in favor of the front seat or the sleeping bag stashed in the bed of his pickup or an empty stall at the—

"I do," she said, interrupting his train of thought.

"Do what?"

"Have a room."

Lust instantly fogged his brain again, shorting any and all remaining thought processes. He could only think of one thing. *She had a room.* "Where?" he growled, barely managing to croak the word out.

"Ah..." The way he was looking at her—as if he wanted to devour her where she stood—had her struggling to remember. "About five miles down the road. West of here. The Broken Spoke Motel."

Without another word, he peeled one of her hands from the sleeve of his shirt, grasped it firmly in his and headed for the glowing red Exit sign on the far side of the dance floor. He plowed through the loud, surging crowd with the single-minded determination of a man hell-bent on getting laid before the night was very much older.

"Hey! Hey, Tom!" A short, bandy-legged cowboy with an energetic dance style stopped mid-twirl, blocking their path. "You comin' back?"

Tom threw him a narrow-eyed look that made the other cowboy grin.

"That mean I need to find myself another ride to Santa Fe?"

"Oh, hell. I forgot." Tom stuffed the first two fingers of his free hand into the front pocket of his jeans and extracted a couple of keys on a ring. He started to toss them to the cowboy, then hesitated and shot a glance at Roxanne. "You got transportation, Slim?"

"A rental car," Roxanne said. "Out front."

Tom nodded and tossed the keys to his grinning buddy. "I'll catch up with you tomorrow in Santa Fe. Don't put any dents in my truck," he ordered as he swept on by the man, towing Roxanne in his wake.

She tripped along behind him, nearly floating, her heart pounding, her knees shaking, her breath sloughing in and out of her lungs, one single, triumphant, giddy thought uppermost in her mind.

I did it! Oh, my God, I really did it! I got myself a dangerous, good-looking cowboy!

And she knew *exactly* what she wanted to do with him.

3

TOM HAD EVERY INTENTION of keeping a tight rein on himself until they got to the Broken Spoke Motel—he sincerely believed some things rightly belonged behind closed doors, despite that kiss in the bar—but she stumbled on the loose gravel of the parking lot as he dragged her through the warm night air toward the flashy little car she'd pointed out to him. Her small soft breasts pressed against his arm, her rounded hip bumped his, and all his good intentions disappeared in a firestorm of mind-numbing heat. He swung around, braced his hips against the low-slung red sports car and hauled her into his arms. "Com'ere, Slim," he growled, and crushed his mouth down on hers.

Roxanne gave one soft, startled yelp, then melted against his chest like hot wax, reaching up to clutch his shoulders as he pulled her tight against him. His body was like iron against hers. His hands were hard and hot on her back. And his mouth was...oh, his mouth was delicious. Indescribably delicious.

She hadn't really had time to appreciate that first kiss in the bar. It had happened so fast and been over so soon, and she'd been so...well, overwhelmed was the only word that came to mind. But now that he was taking his time she could fully appreciate his skill. Oh, yes, she could *definitely* appreciate his skill.

Her dangerous, good-looking cowboy was a wonderful kisser.

A glorious kisser.

Indisputably the best kisser who'd ever puckered up.

His lips were soft and firm at the same time, both greedy and generous as they plucked and nibbled and sucked at hers. Not too wet. Not too dry. Just moist and hot and absolutely perfect, all passion and impatience and wild intemperate lust, with no thought for rules or propriety or her good-girl reputation. She was being ruthlessly, ravenously, thoroughly kissed by a man who knew exactly how it should be done.

It was one of her most cherished fantasies come to life.

With a little sigh of pure unadulterated pleasure, Roxanne wound her arms around his neck to pull herself closer, and parted her lips to suck his clever, marauding tongue deeper into her mouth, determined to give as good as she got.

No way was *this* man going to be able to accuse her of being a cold fish. No way was he going to have to ask if she'd come. No way was she going to lie and tell him she had when she hadn't. And no way was she going to censor even the tiniest, most insignificant element of her response to keep from shocking him. She was going to give him her all. Every sigh. Every moan. Every shudder. She was going to match him kiss for kiss, caress for caress, demand for demand. And before it was over, she was going to have *all* her fantasies fulfilled.

Every hot, lascivious scenario she'd ever imagined.

Every wistful romantic daydream.

Every passing erotic thought.

"Everything," she murmured fervidly, the words hot against his lips. "I want everything. Now."

Tom gave a low, ragged groan, like a man mortally wounded, and slid his hands down her back, cupping her tight little buttocks in his palms. "Lord, Slim, you're killing me here," he growled as he lifted her into the V of his splayed thighs.

Roxanne whimpered in helpless delight and squirmed against him with the wild abandon of a buckle bunny out to get herself another notch on her belt. With no more thought than any healthy female animal in heat, she raised her knee, brushing it up along the outside of his denim-clad thigh, and rubbed herself against his leg in a paroxysm of mindless desire.

Tom slid his hand from the rounded curve of her buttock to the back of her bare thigh, lifting and turning her in one smooth movement so that she was sitting on the front fender of the Mustang. The glossy surface was cool against the backs of her thighs; his lean horseman's hips were hot and hard between them. His fingers dug into her flesh, one hand high on her leg, the other still cupped around the curve of her butt. He pulled her forward—one harsh, quick, convulsive movement—so that the crotch of her leopard-print panties was pressed up against the straining fly of his jeans.

All of Roxanne's fantasies suddenly paled into insignificance against the reality of what was happening. No fantasy, no matter how vivid, could have prepared her for his elemental, unrestrained sexuality—or her own recklessly hedonistic response to it. Awash in sensory overload, swamped by the strength and immediacy of her arousal, she forgot all her carefully laid plans for seduction and simply let herself react to the moment. And she had only one thought in mind at that precise moment. One goal. One overwhelming, pulsating, driving need. Shuddering, sighing, her slender arms locked tight around his neck, Roxanne pulled him down with her as she fell back onto the hood of the car beneath his encroaching weight.

They were chest to breast now, their breathing rasping and heavy, their hearts racing, just as they had been in the bar, but now he was between her thighs, his narrow hips moving in a slow, maddening grind that pressed the hard, heavy bulge beneath the fly of his jeans against the rapidly dampening crotch of her panties. His hands were flexing and kneading her buttocks through the denim of her skirt, lifting them to meet each deliberate downward thrust. His mouth was melded to hers, his tongue probing and exploring, devouring, rapacious and utterly devastating.

Roxanne strained against him, one booted ankle locked behind his thigh to hold him to her, her tongue dueling with his, her hands frantic, skimming over the long, hard muscles of his back, over the swelling mounds of his shoulders, searching for a way beneath the soft cotton fabric of his shirt to the flesh beneath. She found bare skin above his shirt collar—warm, satiny, slightly damp—and pressed her glossy red nails into it, making him moan and arch away, lifting his mouth from hers as he drove his hips forward and down.

She slid frantic fingers up over the back of his head to keep him where he was, found his hat in the way and yanked it off, tossing it blindly away so that it flew over the windshield and landed on the floorboard in the front of the car.

He moved one hand up her side, gliding swiftly over a rounded hip and the gentle dip of her waist, skimming the side of one soft breast, over her smooth, bare shoulder, to fist in the soft, tousled hair at her nape. He drew her head back, forcing her body to bow beneath his, instinctively reasserting his control over her, and dragged his open mouth down the long, elegant line of her throat to the tantalizing swell of cleavage revealed by the scooped neck of her blouse.

Roxanne's response was unhesitating, unapologetic, and wildly uninhibited. She clutched his head in both hands and arched under him, pressing her breasts forward, urging him to take more. To take all. To take everything.

He obliged with flattering speed, his mouth open and sucking at the soft flesh of her breast above her blouse. One hand moved down to her bare thigh, then began inching upward again, sliding under the bunched-up hem of her tiny denim skirt. She felt his fingers skimming along the leg opening of her panties, and then they were edging under it, tracing the sensitive crevice at the top of her thigh, touching the soft crinkly hair that covered her mound, moving inexorably toward the throbbing, heated core of her.

She tensed. Breathless. Waiting. Wanting. Her nerves screaming with anticipation. Her body screaming for release.

"How do you like to be touched, Slim?" he murmured, his voice low and heated, just on the edge of ragged. "Slow and easy?" He skimmed her clitoris with his fingertip, gently, like a man lazily strumming a single string on a guitar.

Roxanne gasped as heat forked through her, and rolled her head against the hood of the Mustang, lifting her hips upward, pressing closer, straining.

"Or fast and furious?" He flicked the swelled nubbin of flesh, quickly, as if he were doing hot licks on a banjo string.

Roxanne bucked wildly beneath him and her hips began to piston in silent demand. She was as taut as an expertly coiled rope, the tension in her arched body a palpable thing that held her, quivering and breathless, on the edge of release, needing only the right touch to send her flying.

"Talk to me, Slim," he growled, his head lifted now so he could watch her face as he held her there, trembling on the brink. His eyes were like blue lasers, hot, intense, and focused. "Tell me how you want to be touched."

Roxanne moaned, incoherent with need and excitement, and reached down to grab his hand, intending to direct his fingers to where she most wanted them to be, to show him what she wanted with every fiber of her being.

"No." He resisted the silent demand. "Tell me."

"I...I... Oh. I don't. I can't. I... Oh, please. *Please*. Just touch me. Touch—"

"Well, hot damn, would you look at that." The voice rang out across the parking lot, boisterous and male. "Yahoo! Ride 'em, cowboy!"

The two people sprawled on the hood of the Mustang stiffened, stilled in a frozen tableau of passion rudely interrupted. Tom's hand was under her skirt, inside her leopard-print panties, a millimeter from where she needed it to be. Roxanne's fingers were clamped around his wrist, the nails biting into his flesh in a futile effort to guide him to the right spot.

"Come on, Hank, honey." It was a woman's voice, high-pitched and giggly. "It ain't polite to stare."

"Well, hell, darlin', it ain't polite to do the wild thing in public, either, but—"

"Come *on,* Hank. Let's just go inside. I want to dance."

They could hear Hank grumbling but he went, his boot heels crunching in the gravel as he followed "darlin'" into the honky-tonk. The door to Ed Earl's creaked open, spilling music and light out into the parking lot, then closed again, surrendering the night to the garish pink glow of the flamingos on the roof.

Roxanne bit back a strangled whimper of frustration and loosened her grip on Tom's wrist, hating the loudmouthed cowboy and his giggling girlfriend with her whole heart. She'd been so close. So tantalizing close! All she'd needed was one more second. Just one more measly little second and she knew her good-looking, dangerous cowboy would have taken her all the way to paradise.

Tom swore ripely and withdrew his hand from Roxanne's panties, silently thanking God or whoever was in charge of looking out for damn fools that Hank and his darlin' hadn't come by two minutes later. He'd been that close—*that* close—to unbuttoning the fly of his Wrangler and giving it to her right there on top the car. Two minutes more—hell, less than two minutes!—he'd have been bare-assed, his jeans around his knees, thrusting into her with no more thought for time and place than a stallion covering a mare.

And no cowboy yahooing in the parking lot would have stopped him until he'd gotten them where they both wanted to go.

Even now, it was a near thing. His control—such as it was—wouldn't survive another close encounter. The next time he put his hands on her, he wouldn't stop until both of them were naked, sweaty, and too exhausted to do more than moan in satisfaction. And, damn it, they needed a bed and some privacy for that!

"Come on, Slim." He stepped back and took hold of both her hands, pulling her upright. "Let's get the hell out of here before we get ourselves arrested."

Bemused, befuddled, her body humming with unfulfilled desires, her brain fogged by unsatisfied lust, Roxanne slid obligingly, even eagerly, off the fender of the car—and then just stood there, staring up at him with a soft, besotted expression on her face. Lord, he was good-looking. And sexy. And she wanted him so much. So very much. More than she'd ever wanted anything or anyone in her entire life. She swayed toward him, her face raised, her lips parted, her eyes drifting closed.

He took a quick step back and dropped her hands. "No."

Her eyes snapped open, widened at his abrupt, almost-biting tone.

"We lock lips again and, I swear, I'll hoist you right back up on the hood of this car and finish it," he warned, his voice low and soft and strained. "Every last cowboy in the bar could come tromping out to watch and I wouldn't stop. Not until we were both too tired to move. And maybe not even then."

Roxanne smiled beatifically, thrilled to the core by his ragged admission. "I wouldn't want you to stop," she said, her voice as ragged, as strained, as his. "I didn't want you to stop before."

Tom gulped audibly and his hands fisted at his sides.

The jolt of pure female sexual power that surged through her at that small, telling gesture was utterly intoxicating, adding another layer to her simmering sexual excitement. No man had ever threatened her with ravishment before. No man had ever had to fight to restrain himself from carrying out that threat, either. It made her feel irresistible. Invincible. Intensely, totally female. At that precise moment, good girl Roxanne Archer disappeared completely. In her place was good-time girl Roxy.

And Roxy was hot.

Roxy was itchy.

Roxy wanted a man—*this* man—and didn't care who knew it.

She tilted her head, looking up at him from under provocatively lowered lashes, and gave him the same slow, seductive come-to-mama smile that had drawn him to her in the bar. But this time there was no calculation in it, no planning or plotting. She was acting on pure feminine instinct. "I guess we'd better do as you suggested, then, shouldn't we?" she said, and licked her lips. Slowly.

Tom made a low growling noise and took a careful step back, away from her and the temptation she so blatantly offered.

Roxanne's smile turned positively feline. Her eyes glowed. Without shifting her gaze from his, she reached down with exaggerated slowness and slid the first two fingers of her right hand into the pocket of her skirt.

"The key," she said, and held the plastic Hertz key ring up in front of his face with the key dangling. "To the car," she added, when he just stood there, staring at it as if he'd never seen a key before. "So we can get the hell out of here before we get arrested," she prompted.

When he still made no move to take it, she reached out, hooked the tip of one long red fingernail on the edge of his shirt pocket, pulled it away from his chest and dropped the key inside. "You drive," she said, and then turned and sauntered around the hood of the car to the passenger side, hips swaying seductively, glossy red nails trailing over the glossy red car. She made a show of getting into the car, affording him a leisurely, heart-stopping view of her cleavage as she bent over to pluck his Stetson off the floor mat, snuggling her butt into the soft leather of the seat, adjusting the hem of her minuscule skirt over her bare legs with a languid, caressing gesture, as if she enjoyed the feel of her own fingers on her skin.

Tom stood stock-still, watching her, unable to move, unable to respond, unable to speak, as dumbstruck as a wet-behind-the-ears, peach-fuzz cowboy who'd just been tossed on his head by a bronc and still hadn't got his breath back yet.

She set his Stetson on her head, adjusting it so that it set, low and sexy, over her forehead, then tilted her head and looked up at him from under the brim. The invitation in her eyes was blatant, unashamed, unwavering, with nothing held back, nothing hidden. She smiled seductively, slowly, and licked her lips again.

Damn, she was…she was… Hell, he didn't know *what* she was!

Except gorgeous.

And hot.

And so damned sexy it made his insides ache and his palms sweat.

One look, that's all it had taken. One long, slow, hot-eyed look from a tall, cool glass of water, and he'd wanted to grab and take and possess. He *had* grabbed and taken and—very nearly, anyway—possessed. And that surprised him. Shocked him, actually. He wasn't normally a man with a short fuse. Ask anybody who knew him and they'd tell you Tom Steele was one careful hombre. He took his time. He considered his options. He weighed all the pros and cons. Steady, that was Tom Steele. Not a man to rush off half-cocked, or to get all hot and bothered and lose his head over a pretty little piece of tail.

Except that he had.

He stood there in the parking lot of Ed Earl's, in the pink-neon glow of those ridiculous flamingos, his heart thudding against the wall of his chest, his cock full to bursting against the fly of his jeans, and his hands… Good Lord, his hands were actually trembling.

He unclenched his fists, flexing his fingers like a gunfighter about to take that long walk down the middle of a dusty street, and took a couple of deep, deliberate breaths in a effort to bring down his heart rate. It didn't work.

"Ah, the hell with it," he muttered, and reached for the door handle of the car. The only thing that was going to slow his heart rate was the exhaustion that came after a fast, furious bout of hot, sweaty sex. Maybe.

She turned toward him as he slid behind the wheel, reaching out to run her hand down his arm.

He didn't even look at her. "Keep your hands to yourself, Slim," he ordered, tight-lipped, as he fished around in his shirt pocket for the key. "And don't say a word." He jammed the key into the ignition and gunned the engine to life. "Not a word until we get to the motel."

Roxanne gave a soft gurgle of laughter, a low, throaty sound of feminine triumph and challenge, and settled back into her seat, her hands folded demurely in her lap. It was only five miles to the motel and judging by the rooster tail of dust and gravel he'd left in Ed Earl's parking lot, they'd be there in less than five minutes. She could wait that long. Barely.

4

THE FACADE of the Broken Spoke Motel was cheap Hollywood Western, with an unpainted barn-board exterior, a split-log hitching rail running along the front, and horseshoes bracketing the room numbers on each of the doors. A red-neon wagon wheel, one spoke seeming to swing back and forth as it flashed on and off, sat perched atop a pole in front of the motel office, right above the unblinking No Vacancy sign. A bank of vending machines stood on the cracked concrete apron just outside the office door, in clear sight of whoever was manning the registration desk. At the moment it was empty, with a hand-lettered sign advising would-be guests to ring for assistance.

Tom pulled into the first open parking space in the lot, jammed on the parking brake, and was out of the car almost before the engine stopped idling. His boot heels sent up little puffs of dust as he rounded the hood, purpose in every deliberate step, burning lust in his eyes, one thing on his mind. Roxanne sat in the passenger seat in stupefied delight and watched him come to her, come *after* her, thrilled beyond belief to be the object of such single-minded desire. With a sense of delighted amazement, she realized she could actually feel her nipples, rigid against the satiny fabric of her leopard-print bra, could feel the wetness soaking the matching fabric between her legs, could feel the blood pounding through her veins. She had never been so aware of her body, never felt so sensitized, so aroused, as if every nerve ending was on red alert. She was tingling all over...her lips...her fingertips...her thighs...every part of her quivering with anticipation and wanton, intemperate need, making her wonder how she was going to manage to stand up and walk to the room without collapsing into a quivering heap at his feet.

She didn't have to try.

He yanked open the door and bent down, scooping her up into his arms. "Which room?" he growled as he shoved the door closed with his foot.

It was another cherished fantasy fulfilled. Being swept off her feet. Carried off to be ravaged by a dangerous cowboy. The old Roxanne would have likely fainted from excitement; the new Roxy looped her arms around her cowboy's neck and tickled his ear with her tongue, as if being swept off her feet were an every day occurrence.

Tom's whole body tensed at her teasing caress, and his hands tightened on her thighs and back as a spasm of sheer sexual pleasure shot through him. If he didn't get inside her in the next sixty seconds he was going to come in his jeans. And that hadn't happened since he was fourteen. "Which room, Slim?"

"Seven." She sighed the word into his ear, her breath hot and moist. "Lucky seven." She slid her tongue down the side of his neck, and then up again, as if he were her favorite flavor of ice cream and she was intent on savoring every last delicious drop. "Second door past the office."

Tom turned on his heel and headed toward the promise of paradise with long ground-eating strides, while the woman in his arms did her best to drive him to his knees before they got there. He stumbled slightly when she stuck her tongue in his ear, but managed to regain his balance with a quick, light-footed move that brought him to a halt directly in front of the trio of vending machines in front of the motel office. One offered the usual soft drinks, another candy bars and chips, the third had toiletries for sale…miniature tubes of toothpaste, tins of aspirin, palm-size packets of tissue, condoms. A mental picture of his battered canvas carryall, still stowed behind the front seat of his pickup, flashed through his mind.

Roxanne left off nibbling on his earlobe to raise her head. "What?" she murmured, her eyes wide and hazy with arousal, her voice softly slurred.

Tom indicated the offerings in the vending machine with a jerk of his chin. "Am I going to need those?"

Her arms still locked securely around his neck, Roxanne glanced over her shoulder to see what he was talking about. "I've got one inside my bra."

His eyes blazed. "Only one?"

"And a whole box in my room," she assured him. "There are a dozen in it. Well—" she loosened her hold on him with one hand and touched the little foil packet of protection tucked inside her push-up bra, inadvertently drawing his eyes to the creamy mounds of flesh above the neckline of her blouse "—eleven,

anyway,'' she managed, watching his eyes heat and
burn.

"A dozen just might do it. Maybe." He bent his
head and nuzzled the scented valley between her
plumped-up breasts, breathing her in with a long hungry gulp of air. "Or maybe not," he said softly, the
breath rushing out of him in a tremulous sigh.

And, just like that, Roxanne fell a little bit in love.
Not the happily-ever-after, till-death-do-us-part kind
of love. She wasn't that much of a fool. But it was
love, nonetheless, a light-headed, lighthearted, giddy
kind of love, as insubstantial as moonbeams and neon,
as temporary as the victory after a championship
bronc ride. But it made what was about to happen just
that much more wonderful and exciting. More thrilling. More everything. If she hadn't already been dewy
with need, that one sweet, tender gesture would have
done it.

"Hurry," she whispered, and nipped his earlobe for
emphasis. *"Hurry."*

Tom hurried.

"The key?" he said, letting her slide down his
body as he set her on her feet in front of the door to
room number seven.

"That's in my bra, too."

"Get it."

She leaned against the door, her hands behind her
back, her breasts thrust out, and looked up at him from
beneath the brim of his hat. "Why don't you get—"

"No." It was the same abrupt tone he'd used in
the parking lot when he'd backed off from kissing her.
But this time he didn't back off. He simply stood

there, looking down at her with hot dangerous lights dancing in his blue eyes. ''I'm on the thin edge of control here, Slim, and if I put my hand down your blouse now, I'm going to end up fucking you where you stand, right here against this door, in front of God and everybody. Is that what you want?''

She almost said yes. The word hovered on the tip of her tongue for a dangerous moment, enticing them both with the possibility of flagrant debauchery. And then Tom put his hands on her shoulders, jerked her away from the door, and turned her around. ''Get the key, Slim, and open the damned door.''

Roxanne fumbled for the key, fumbled as she fit it into the lock, fumbled as she turned the doorknob and stepped over the threshold. She should be aghast, she knew. Ashamed of her lack of control. Appalled at her willingness to make a public spectacle of herself. Yesterday, she would have been. Maybe tomorrow, she would be again. But right now, she wasn't. Couldn't be. Right now, she was on fire, burning up from the inside out, trembling with desire. The only thing on her mind, the single driving thought in her head, was the overwhelming need to assuage the heat, to quench the aching desire, to find sweet release with her good-looking, dangerous cowboy.

And then the door crashed closed behind her, and his arm encircled her waist, and he spun her around, crushing his mouth to hers, and she ceased to think at all.

He propelled her backward toward the bed, his mouth fastened to hers, feasting, his hands moving over her body, frantically molding her breasts and back and the sweet, subtle curve of her bottom through her clothes. Her kisses were as greedy, as wildly intemperate as his, her hands as frantic, touching him everywhere she could reach. The backs of her knees hit the edge of the bed and she tumbled onto it, pulling him down on top of her. They bounced once, sending the cowboy hat she still wore somersaulting over the edge of the mattress to the floor. Entwined like tangled kudzu vines, they rolled across the bed and crashed into the headboard. It banged against the wall and they rolled away, mouths still hotly fused, hands still moving frantically, bodies pressed together, legs entangled, hips grinding together. Tom's foot hit the rickety bedside table, causing the equally rickety bedside lamp to wobble on its base, sending shadows flickering precariously across the walls and ceiling, counterpoint to the intermittent flash of red neon from the motel sign pulsing through the slanted blinds on the window.

Neither one of them paid it any heed. Neither of them would have noticed if the lamp had gone crashing to the floor. The only thing that registered was the searing wildfire need that ricocheted back and forth between them, the only thing that mattered was satisfying that need.

Immediately.

Now.

Tom shoved both hands under her tiny denim skirt, pushing it up to her waist, and curled his fingers under the low-slung waistband of her leopard-print panties. And then he paused, still on the thin edge of control, and stared down into her wide, whiskey-colored eyes.

She stared back at him, her gaze avid, unwavering, and unabashedly eager, without coyness or equivocation, primed and ready for whatever came next.

"This first time is going to be a fast, hard ride," he said, his voice low and guttural. "If that's not what you want, say so now."

She bent her knees, planting her boot heels on the edge of the mattress, and lifted her hips. "It's what I want."

He yanked her panties off, tugging them past her raised hips, dragging them down her legs, wrestling them over her boots, and tossed them on the floor. His hands went to his fly, his fingers working frantically at the metal buttons to free his erection as he slid his body back up between her legs. He grasped her bare thighs, his strong callused fingers digging into her flesh as he spread them wider, meaning to drive himself into her, hard and fast the way they both wanted, to take her with elemental, unthinking fury.

But something about the way she lay there, her minuscule skirt pushed up around her waist, her bent knees splayed, her soft, hot, woman's body open and vulnerable to his every desire, had him suddenly gentling his approach. She was so pretty and fragile there between her legs, all plump and pink and glistening, with the feeble light from the bedside lamp glinting on the smooth pale skin of her thighs, and the red neon pulsing like a heartbeat, giving her an all-over rosy glow. The soft blond hair between her legs had been waxed or shaved or whatever it was that women did, into a narrow little rectangle that barely covered her mound. It was rawly sexy, and inexplicably, elegantly refined. Just as she was.

He softened his grip and slid his palms down the inside of her thighs, slowly, caressingly, until his thumbs just touched her vulva. Her body jerked beneath him, a tiny involuntary movement that could have signaled rejection or acceptance of his intimate invasion. He raised his gaze to her face again. She stared back through the frame of her splayed knees, her lips moist and parted, her cheeks flushed, the expression in her eyes as soft, as hot, as open and vulnerable as her body.

Slowly, still holding her gaze with his, he slid his thumbs down and then up, then down again—once, twice, three times—gently skimming her most sensitive flesh. Her body undulated, like a field of ripe wheat rippling in the wind, and she uttered a breathy little sound, half moan, half sigh, that shuddered out between her lips.

"You're wet." His voice was low and caressing, his gaze voracious and admiring. "Hot and wet and slippery."

"Yes." She didn't blush. Didn't look away. "I am."

"I want you wetter. I want you—" he moved his thumbs inward a fraction of an inch, pressing down, closing in, capturing her distended clitoris between them in a sensuous little squeeze play "—dripping."

Her body tightened, straining, and the sound she made was definitely a moan. A deep, throaty, on-the-edge moan.

He eased his thumbs back a teasing fraction of an

inch from her slick swollen center and watched her
eyes flare wide in mindless entreaty, watched her bite
her lip against protest and plea. Her desire was palpable, her anticipation a living, breathing thing between them.

He knew exactly what she wanted.

Needed.

Had to have.

In another mood, he might have made her say the
words, might have teased her—and himself—by making her ask for what she wanted. Instead, he slid his
hands under her hips, slid his body down off the bed
until his knees were on the floor and his shoulders
were wedged between her thighs.

''We'll save the hard riding for later,'' he said, and
buried his face between her legs.

Roxanne nearly levitated off the bed at the first
heated, silken stroke of his tongue against her throbbing clitoris. Her back arched like a bow. Her hands
clutched at the worn chenille bedspread, gathering it
into her clenched fists. Her booted heels pressed down
into the edge of the mattress. She moaned. Loudly.
And then more loudly still as he brought his fingers
into play again, opening her more fully to his lasciviously talented tongue.

It felt as if every nerve ending in her body began
and ended in that one tiny nubbin of sensitized flesh
between her legs. She throbbed. She ached. She vi-
brated with need. And, then, in a blinding, incandes-
cent blaze of sheer primal lust, she came. It was gut-
wrenching. Breath-stealing. Mind-blowing.

Sublime.

"More," she demanded, when her breath finally shuddered back into her lungs and she could breathe again. She released her death grip on the bedspread and reached down, fisting her hands in his dark, silky hair, pressing him closer, straining for another peak. "More."

He acquiesced with satisfying gallantry and greed, with no hint of hesitation or resistance, as if continuing to pleasure her with his mouth had been his intention all along. And, maybe, it had been. She was sweet and tender, so incredibly hot and responsive that it was pure, unadulterated pleasure to give her what she wanted. Because it was what he wanted, too.

Making her scream with ecstasy had been high on his list of priorities since the first moment he'd seen her in the bar. He'd thought to do it by pounding her into the mattress. He still meant to do it that way. Later. Right now, he was determined to tease those screams of ecstasy out of her with his tongue. She'd uttered that one, long, shuddering, gasping breath when she came the first time; he wanted a full-throated scream the next time she went over. He slipped his hands back under her bare squirming bottom to hold her more securely, and set about getting what he wanted with the same single-minded focus he applied to everything.

In minutes, he had her writhing between his hands. Her hips undulated against his mouth in mindless entreaty. Her head thrashed against the bed. Her breath came in throaty little whimpers and panting moans, interspersed with disjointed pleas and fragmented demands.

"Oh, God... I... Yes. Oh, yes. There. Oh, please. Yes. Right there. Yes. Yes. *Yes!*"

The last yes came out as a strangled shout, a muffled scream that barely echoed off the thin walls of the motel room.

Satisfied with that, Tom lifted his head and pressed a soft kiss to the soft crinkly hair that covered her mound.

"Inside," she demanded raggedly, nearly delirious with need. She yanked on his hair, trying to pull him up her body. "I need you inside me. Now. Right *now.*"

Tom didn't have to be asked twice. He levered himself on top of her with a supple shift of his body, sliding up between her splayed thighs. His engorged penis nudged her slick folds, seeking the entrance to her soft, hot woman's body. It took every ounce of his considerable willpower to keep from plunging into her. Instead, calling upon his last reserves of control, he pushed himself up onto his knees and reached for the top button on her blouse.

"The condom." The words were gritted out between clenched teeth. His hands were trembling. "Where's the damned condom?"

Roxanne pushed his groping hands away to retrieve it herself. "I'll do it," she said, curling the foil-wrapped packet into her fist when he would have taken it from her. "I want to do it."

"Then do it," he ordered. *"Quick."*

With hands that were surprisingly steady given the raging storm going on inside of her, she peeled the two halves of the foil wrapping back, tossed it aside, and reached down with both hands to sheath him. His penis was incredibly hot to the touch. Incredibly hard. She curled her fingers around his steely, latex-shielded length and guided him into her.

"Ride me, cowboy." The words were a demand. A plea. A prayer. "Ride me hard."

He drove himself into her with all the finesse of a sex-crazed adolescent mounting his first woman. His body was tense and quivering, muscles straining, hips pistoning wildly, madly, almost violently. Pounding into her, taking her, possessing her, riding her. Hard. Roxanne cried out, a feral sound of surrender and triumph both, and drove her hips upward, meeting him thrust for thrust. It was hot and wild. Untamed. Uncivilized. Out of control. Damp flesh slamming into damp flesh...breathing hot and labored...long callused fingers digging into soft giving flesh...long red nails pressing into hard straining muscles...lips parted, gasping for air...eyes closed tight to better savor the battering maelstrom of sensation...relentlessly driving each other to completion.

The mattress creaked beneath them, counterpoint to each powerful thrust. The headboard banged against the wall. The lamp wobbled on its stand. And still they hammered at each other, striving, straining, battling toward the ultimate peak of physical sensation.

And then all of Roxanne's small inner muscles began to spasm. Hard. Fast. Unstoppable. Inevitable. The movement spread outward, tightening the muscles in her belly and back and thighs, drawing her nipples into stiff aching buds, arching her body up off of the bed until she was as taut as a quivering bow.

Tom thrust into her twice more—deeply, powerfully, heavily—deliberately pushing her over the edge. She fell with a high keening cry, trilling her satisfaction and pleasure with the same lack of restraint she'd shown in going after it in the first place.

With a hard convulsive shudder, he let go and went over himself. The feeling began between his legs, pulling everything tight and hard, nearly painful in its intensity, radiating outward in pulsating waves that curled his toes inside his battered Tony Lamas and nearly caused his eyes to roll back in his head.

They collapsed onto each other, *into* each other in a boneless heap, trembling and damp, wrung out, replete, utterly satisfied. Several minutes passed in silence as they lay there, panting, still entwined, still intimately joined, and waited for the world to right itself around them.

Roxanne surfaced by slow degrees, the sensual haze clouding her mind dissipating bit by bit as she came back to herself. She could feel the hard round shape of his belt buckle pressing into the soft flesh of her inner thigh, feel the pearl snaps on his shirt pressing into her breasts and belly through the thin cotton fabric of her eyelet blouse. His breath was hot against her neck. His hands still cupped her bare bottom. His penis was still snug inside of her. He was a dead weight on top of her, a hundred and eighty pounds of exhausted, hard-muscled male, but she lay there quietly beneath him for several long contented minutes, her body deliciously relaxed and sated, and deliberately took stock of the situation.

Common sense would dictate that she should be

feeling ashamed, or guilty, or at least foolish about what she had just done. Instead, she was absurdly pleased with herself. Good-girl Roxanne Archer had picked up a good-looking, dangerous cowboy in a tacky honky-tonk, taken him back to her tacky motel room, and had wild, raunchy sex with him. Nobody back in Connecticut would believe it. She could hardly believe it herself. And, yet, there she was, spread-eagled and flat on her back beneath said cowboy, still wallowing in the afterglow of a monumental, toe-curling, mind-bending orgasm—and thinking about doing it again as soon as humanly possible. Or as soon as they both got their breaths back.

She smoothed her hand down the long damp curve of his spine, under the pale blue shirt he still wore, to the hard swell of his bare buttock. "I don't mean to complain, sugar." She patted his fanny lightly, appreciatively. "But you're smashing me flat."

He grunted, a purely male sound that delighted her feminine soul, and levered himself up onto his elbows to relieve her of most of his weight. His head hung down between his shoulders, as if it were too heavy to lift just yet, his face still buried in the curve of her neck. She could feel his eyelashes, soft as butterfly wings, flutter against her skin as he opened his eyes, and then he raised his head and gave her a slow, sexy, self-satisfied smile.

"You get the license number of the truck that hit us?"

Roxanne smiled back, pleased and gratified by the implication that she wasn't the only one who been broadsided by the big O. "What truck was that, sugar?'' she said playfully, and fluttered her eyelashes at him.

"Big ol' eighteen-wheeler roarin' down the highway at ninety miles an hour, at least. Knocked the stuffing right out of me.''

"Oh, I don't know. You still feel pretty—'' she made a little thrusting motion with her hips "—stuffed to me.''

Tom's smile widened into a teasing, lopsided grin. "You've got your anatomy wrong, Slim. You're the one who's—'' he countered the teasing movement of her hips with a quick thrusting movement of his own "—stuffed.''

Roxanne's appreciative chuckle turned into a low throaty moan. Her hands tightened on the cheeks of his butt. Her back arched.

And, just like that, he was rock-hard again, as hot and horny and hungry as if he hadn't just exhausted himself between her thighs. His teasing grin faded. The lazy glow in his eyes sharpened and focused. He pushed himself up onto his hands, pressing her hips more deeply into the mattress, and stared down at her, incredulous and amazed. He was thirty-one years old, for God's sake! He wasn't supposed to be ready for Round Two so soon.

"This is crazy," he murmured, fighting the urge to begin thrusting like a wild man again. "*We're* crazy. You know that, don't you? Completely crazy.''

"Yes." She tightened her hands on his backside, trying to press him closer, deeper. "I know. Crazy."

"We're both of us still half dressed." He gave in to temptation, and the silent demand of her hands on his butt, and rotated his hips, grinding his pubis against hers. "Still got our boots on."

"Yes," she agreed. "Boots. We should take our boots off and— Oh! Oh, yes." The word was a long drawn-out hosanna of inarticulate appreciation. "Do that again."

"I don't even know your name." He made another small, deliberate grinding motion. "You don't know mine."

"I know your name." The words fluttered out in little panting breaths. "Your name is Tom Steele. And mine is Roxan—Roxy," she corrected, catching herself. "Roxy Arch— Oh, yes! Again. Please." She wrapped her legs around his waist, locking her booted ankles at the small of his back to keep him inside her when he started to withdraw. *"Again!"* she demanded.

He did it again.

And then again.

Very slowly.

Very deliberately.

Very gently.

Roxanne bucked beneath him, her hips pistoning as she tried to increase the pace, and the pressure. "Faster," she panted. "Harder. Oh, please. *Harder.*"

He gave in to one demand and resisted the other, pressing down harder, while at the same time restricting the movement of her hips with his until they were barely moving at all.

"Take it easy, Slim." The words were low and soft, gritted out through clenched teeth as he struggled to resist her passionate demands and the inclinations of his own body. He wanted it to last a good long while this time, and that wasn't going to happen if he let go and started thrusting like a madman. "Real slow and easy," he murmured, suiting words to action as he ground his pelvis against hers. "Let's make it last this time."

Roxanne uttered an inarticulate protest and strained against him, her legs clamped around him like a vise, her thighs and belly taut and quivering, her back arched, her teeth clamped over her lower lip as she fought to take what he held just out of her reach.

"Easy," he said, and ducked his head, brushing his mouth over hers, skimming his tongue over her abused lip. "Take it easy. Just let go and take it easy. We'll get there."

He continued to rotate his pelvis against hers, his engorged penis rock-hard and motionless inside her, his pubic bone pressing against her clitoris in a tiny, focused, unrelentingly gentle motion that seemed to go on forever, winding her tighter and tighter, like barbed wire being slowly, carefully tightened with a winch, stretching every muscle and nerve ending to the very edge of release, holding her there until she gave in and went limp beneath him, letting him take her where he would.

He rose, then, catching her legs in the crook of his elbows as they slid bonelessly from around his waist. He leaned forward, pulling her legs high and wide, opening her fully, and placed his hands on the bed beside her shoulders. And, finally, he began to thrust. Deep and slow at first, long, deliberate strokes that gradually—oh, so very gradually!—became faster and harder as she began to writhe beneath him.

Faster.

Harder.

Faster.

Harder.

Until, suddenly, it was too much and too hard and too fast, and everything broke loose in a wild, uncontrollable whirlwind of nearly unbearable sensation, like a hundred strands of bared wire that had snapped under intolerable pressure.

She screamed this time. It was a full-throated, unselfconscious scream of triumphant release that had the occupants of the neighboring room pounding on the wall and demanding quiet. Ignoring their demands, Tom uttered his own exultant shout of satisfaction and followed her into the spinning vortex.

"Next time," he promised, just before he collapsed on top of her, "we'll get our boots off first."

ROXANNE WAS DEFINITELY sans boots when she woke up the next morning. She was also sans everything else, including blankets of any kind. She lay on her side on the rumpled bed, her knees drawn up, her naked flesh pebbling under the arctic blast of the air-conditioning unit in the window. Bright Texas sunlight glittered through the slatted blinds, creating a ladder-like pattern on the worn carpet, over the scattered articles of clothing and bed linens that littered the floor, and across the broad golden back of the naked man lying in bed beside her.

Her good-looking dangerous cowboy hadn't disappeared with the morning's light as she'd half feared he might, but lay facedown, taking up a full three-quarters of the motel bed, snoring ever so softly into his pillow.

Roxanne couldn't help the idiotic grin that spread across her face at the sight of him. She also couldn't stop herself from reaching out to run her hand over all that glorious masculine pulchritude. She would have thought she'd have gotten enough of him sometime during the long, sweaty, tempestuous night that had gone before, but she hadn't. If anything, last night had only made her want more. More touching. More kissing. More of him. More of herself the way she was with him.

She'd never been so uninhibited. Never been so voracious and greedy. Never been so effortlessly responsive. It was a side of herself she hadn't previously known existed and she wanted to explore it.

At length.

In depth.

Right now.

She tiptoed her fingers back up his spine and tickled the nape of his neck.

He stirred beneath her touch, the long lean muscles of his back flexing, the smooth rounded muscles of his shoulders bunching ever so slightly under his golden skin as he turned his head toward her. He blinked owlishly, not quite all there. "I wasn't sure you'd be here this morning," he said.

Her fingers stilled. "Are you disappointed that I am?"

"Lord, no!" He rolled to his side, levering himself

up onto his elbow, catching her hand before she could draw it away. "I thought maybe I'd dreamed you, is all."

"Then I must have been dreaming, too."

He grinned. "Hell of a dream," he said, and lifted her captured hand to his lips for a quick kiss. "I hate to see it end."

"Who says it has to?" she said, and felt her heart flutter at the audacity of what she was about to suggest.

"Don't you have someplace you have to be?" He cocked an eyebrow at her. "A home? A job? Something?" He hesitated. "Someone?" he suggested.

"Nope. I'm free as a bird for the rest of the summer. There's nowhere I have to be until September. No one I'm accountable to." She looked up at him from under the veil of her lashes. "You interested?"

"In?" he said carefully, not quite sure she was suggesting what he thought he was suggesting. No man could be *that* lucky.

"You. Me." She tugged her hand out of his, slid it down his torso, curled it around his penis. It hardened instantly, filling her hand to overflowing. "This." She squeezed him lightly. "All. Summer. Long."

Tom nearly swallowed his tongue. He had to consciously tell himself to take a breath before he could speak. "And when the summer's over?"

"When the summer's over, we go our separate ways. No fuss. No muss. No strings. And no looking back."

Good God Almighty, Tom thought, as what she said

sank in. He'd just been offered a last fling that was going to take him nearly to the end of the rodeo season. And then she'd disappear from his life. A man *could* be that lucky!

"So, how about it, sugar?" She squeezed him more firmly, adding a leisurely up-and-down stroke for good measure. "You want to take me on for the rest of the summer?"

5

THE DRIVE from the Broken Spoke Motel in Lubbock, Texas, to the rodeo grounds in Santa Fe, New Mexico, was nearly eight hours long, which gave Roxanne more than enough time to think about what she'd done the night before—and what she'd agreed to do for the remaining two and a half months of her summer vacation.

The first was an event she had planned for as carefully and completely as she did her class curriculum each year. Like the thorough, conscientious, obsessively good girl she was, she'd considered her options, made her decision, then spent a good six months laying the groundwork for getting laid. She'd taken country-western dance lessons, researched the rodeo, read every sex manual, erotic novel and women's magazine article on attracting and seducing the male of the species that she could get her hands on. From there, it had taken nearly a week of attending rodeos to decide on the cowboy she wanted. And then another week of careful study to transform herself into the kind of woman he might conceivably want in return.

The second event, however, was a decision her sexy alter ego had made on the spur of the moment, in the heat of passion, so to speak. And Roxanne wasn't entirely sure if she was comfortable with that decision. Could she *be* Roxy for two and a half months? Could conservative, stick-in-the-mud, good girl Roxanne Archer sustain the transformation to good-time girl Roxy without reverting to type and blowing her cover? Did she have the stamina and the cunning to stay in character for that long? More importantly, did she have the wardrobe?

She'd only planned on a weekend of sexual excess—a week, if she got really lucky—and had purchased accordingly. A pair of cowboy boots, one denim miniskirt, a pair of jeans, a couple of skimpy tops and some sexy new underwear weren't going to last her an entire summer. If she was going to do this—and, she realized, she *was* going to do it, was *already* doing it, despite the misgivings still niggling at the back of her mind—she needed to supplement her new wardrobe. Otherwise, she'd be reduced to wearing the khaki slacks and linen camp shirts that were her usual summer uniform. And that wouldn't suit Roxy, at all.

"Having second thoughts?"

Roxanne hooked a strand of flying hair behind her ear with one long red nail and looked over at her good-looking, dangerous cowboy. He sat in the driver's seat of her rented convertible, his left elbow on the car door, his right wrist draped over the steering wheel, his hat pulled down low over his eyes, piloting the car down the long, lonely ribbon of highway at speeds that just begged a cop to stop them. If there had been any cops, that is. She hadn't seen anything besides the occasional eighteen-wheeler for miles.

"I beg your pardon?" she said politely, and then belatedly remembered her San Antonio drawl. She fluttered her eyelashes to cover the lapse. "You say something, sugar?"

"You've been sitting over there, lost in thought for the past thirty minutes. I was wondering if you were having second thoughts."

"Second thoughts about what?"

"About us." He flicked the hand he had draped over the steering wheel, the gesture eloquent in spite of its brevity. "This."

"I never have second thoughts," Roxanne said airily, lying through her teeth.

Roxanne *always* had second thoughts. And third and fourth ones, too. But she was sure Roxy didn't. Roxy was a decisive, daring, devil-may-care, fly-by-the-seat-of-her-pants kind of girl; the kind of girl careful, conservative Roxanne had always secretly envied.

"Once I make a decision—bam—" she snapped her fingers in the air between them "—it's made. Second thoughts are a waste of time. Unless..." She felt her stomach clench as one of those second thoughts she denied having popped into her mind. "Are *you* having second thoughts, sugar?" She shot him a sliding sideways glance, rife with deliberate insouciance in case he was. "Because, if you are, we can dissolve this—" she ran her fingernail along the top of his thigh "—partnership—" she said, encouraged when his quads tensed "—at the next truck stop. You just say the word and I'll be gone. No muss, no fuss, re-member?''

She patted his thigh and lifted her hand, only to find it captured beneath his. He drew it to his crotch, pressing it down over the rapidly hardening bulge beneath his fly. ''Does that feel like I'm having second thoughts?''

Roxanne's cherry-red lips turned up in a wicked smile of pure feminine satisfaction—and relief. ''It sure feels like you're having some kind of thoughts.'' She squeezed him lightly. ''You want to stop some-where and act on those thoughts, sugar?''

His smile was as wicked as hers. ''I wasn't thinking about stopping at all,'' he said, and moved her hand in a suggestive up-and-down motion before releasing it.

Roxanne felt an illicit thrill zing through her. Here was another fantasy, hers for the taking, if she dared. She'd never done what he was suggesting, not in a moving vehicle. Not in a vehicle at all, actually. Not anywhere. The world of lovers' lanes and teenage sex in the back seat of Daddy's car hadn't been one she'd ever been invited to enter. There had been no heavy petting in somebody's rec room or fogging up the windows in a parked car. She'd been nearly twenty-four, a responsible adult with a job and her own apart-ment when she surrendered her virginity. By then, there had been no need for furtive sex or forbidden thrills. She'd always wondered what she'd missed. What it would be like to indulge in frenzied sex acts that stopped short of intercourse.

Now was her chance to find out.

She couldn't resist.

Didn't *want* to resist.

Feeling decadent and daring, she squeezed him slowly, leisurely, measuring the length and hardness of his erection beneath her palm. He was satisfyingly hard, deliciously long, gloriously thick. She made a purring sound in her throat and tiptoed her fingers up the straining bulge to the metal button at the top of his fly.

His stomach muscles contracted.

She flicked the button open.

He drew in a quick, hard breath.

She grasped the waistband of his jeans between her thumb and forefinger and gave a sharp little tug. The remaining buttons of his fly popped open, one after the other, slowly—pop, pop, pop—each one a tiny explosion of sound that was more felt than heard. Without giving herself a chance to chicken out, she flattened her palm against his washboard stomach, slid her fingertips under the elastic edge of his briefs, and burrowed down between his legs.

His breath hissed out between clenched teeth and he shifted in his seat, spreading his knees to accommodate her and give her room to explore.

She caressed his balls, cupping them gently in her palm for a delicious moment, and then curled her fingers around his hot, rigid flesh, and began a slow squeezing stroking meant to drive him mad.

He seemed to swell in her hand, becoming harder and longer and thicker with each stroke. He had both hands on the wheel, now, his knuckles white with the ferocity of his grip. His breathing was fast and shallow. His upper lip was beaded with sweat. His foot was a lead weight on the accelerator.

Roxanne was surprised to find her excitement matching his. Her breathing was fast and shallow. Her pulse was racing. Her body was tingling. She hadn't realized it would be like that, hadn't imagined that being the seducer would be as thrilling as being seduced. She felt incredibly powerful, incredibly sexual, incredibly female.

She wanted—desperately—to make him come with just her hands alone.

She released her seat belt and shifted in her seat, twisting her body sideways so she could reach over the console with her right hand and cup his balls through his jeans. With her left, she continued the long squeezing strokes, using her thumb to spread the pearl of moisture that appeared at the tip of his penis and increase the friction, moving her fist faster and faster as she felt his tension build.

Tom stiffened and made a low, guttural sound deep in his throat. The car swerved, the back end fishtailing wildly, spewing up gravel as he steered it onto the shoulder of the road and stomped on the brakes. Roxanne's body was propelled forward, and then back against the seat, but her rhythm never faltered. She was intent on one thing, and one thing only, and wasn't stopping until she got it.

And then it happened.

With his hands tight on the steering wheel, his arms rigid, his boot heels pressed against the floor, his head pressed back into the headrest, Tom uttered a harsh, rasping cry, and erupted in a spectacular orgasm. Roxanne watched it happen, entranced and enthralled.

She had done that.

She had made him lose control.

She had made him come.

She felt triumphant. Exultant. Victorious. Smug.

"Your turn," he said, and grabbed her by the shoulders, dragging her across the console to sprawl awkwardly in his lap. She lay on her side, her upper body wedged between his chest and the steering wheel, her hip balanced on the console between the seats, her booted feet against the passenger door. His mouth came down on hers, hot and hard and ravaging. His hand went between her legs, rubbing her through the heavy seam of her jeans. That was all it took. She was already wet, already aroused, drunk on passion and power and the excitement of the new and forbidden. She came hard, her body arching, her nails digging into the hard curve of his shoulders, her thighs clamped tight over his hand. It didn't stop his fingers from moving, though. He drove her up again, and then yet again, until she was quivering in his arms, until she was shivering and panting and making gasping little whimpering sounds, begging him to please, please fuck her. He brought both hands up to her head, then, cradling it between his wide callused palms, and gentled his kiss, going from ravager to protector in an instant.

His lips plucked at hers, softly, moist and tender, raining kisses to soothe them both, easy, gentle caresses that fell on her lips and cheeks and eyelids, meant to cool their roiling passions and take them to a place where they could draw an even breath. She sighed tremulously, her breath catching like a child who's cried too hard and too long, and melted into his arms, tucking her hot face into the damp curve of his neck while he stroked her temple with his thumb and drew soothing little circles on the back of her head with his fingertips.

They stayed that way for several long minutes, just holding each other, quietly, coming down off the edge together, until an eighteen-wheeler rolled by, buffeting the little convertible with its passing, blowing a long, loud salute on its air horn. Roxanne put her hands against his shoulders and pushed, squirming backward into her own seat. Tom levered his hips up slightly, reaching into his back pocket for the bandana he always carried. He cleaned himself with it, then folded it and passed it to Roxanne to wipe her hands while he rearranged and rebuttoned.

"It's nearly lunchtime," he said, after they had set themselves to rights. "You hungry?"

"I could eat, I guess," she said, without quite meeting his eyes.

She was a little embarrassed, now that it was over. It was, after all, one thing to have wild raucous sex in the relative privacy of an anonymous motel room. It was quite another to jerk a man off in an open convertible at high noon on the side of the highway. She couldn't help but wonder if she had crossed the line from good-time girl to, well…slut.

"There's a truck stop a few miles up the road, just the other side of Tucumari. Pete's Eats. They've got great burritos. That sound okay to you?"

Roxanne nodded. "Sounds fine," she said, and leaned down, snagging her purse off the floor. She began rooting around in it, ignoring him.

Tom knew by the way she was acting that he had fallen short somewhere. That he hadn't done or said whatever the right thing was to do or say in a situation like this. But, damn, he'd never had a woman do that to him, not in an open car, speeding down the highway. Not while he wasn't busy returning the favor. He hadn't expected her to do it, either. His gesture had just been a tease. A dare. He'd expected her to give him a little squeeze through his jeans, a little pat, maybe make some risqué comment about holding his horses until a more appropriate time.

But then she'd unbuttoned his fly and taken him in her hot little hand, and all his expectations were shot to hell in an explosion of panting lust and excitement that was fueled as much by *how* she did what she did, as *what* she did. She'd been avid and intent, her excitement as hot and palpable as his. He'd never had a woman give that way, completely unselfishly, focused on his pleasure alone and asking nothing in return until he'd dragged her into his lap and made her beg.

Tom didn't know what the hell to say to that, how to act. He felt gauche and grateful, and totally inadequate, like the callow inexperienced boy he hadn't been for many years. Knowing he had to do something, say something to let her know what her actions meant to him, he reached over and captured her chin, interrupting her careful application of a fresh coat of lipstick as he turned her to face him.

"You're something else, Slim," he said softly, his tone admiring and appreciative and awed. "Damn, you are just something fucking else."

Roxanne smiled beatifically, her confidence restored, and pursed her lips in a ripe, red air kiss.

THEY HAD A QUICK LUNCH of beans and burritos at Pete's Eats and took their coffee in to-go cups to save time and get back on the road more quickly. Roxanne added a precise half teaspoon of sugar to hers, stirring it thoroughly to make sure it dissolved.

"Why bother?" Tom said, watching her as she daintily tapped her spoon on the edge of the cup and set it, bowl down, on the corner of a paper napkin.

"Because that's the way I like it," she said, and snapped the plastic lid on with a firm click. She picked her purse up, slung it over her shoulder and held her hand out, palm up. "Key, please," she said, and wriggled her fingers imperiously.

Tom covered his shirt pocket with the flat of his hand. "You got some objection to my driving?"

"Nope." She reached over and slid her fingers into his pocket, snagging the key ring with the tip of her fingernail. "It's my turn to drive, is all."

"This is Texas, Slim," he said as he followed her out to the car. "Real men don't let women drive 'em around in Texas. It ain't manly."

"In case you didn't notice, cowboy, we crossed the border into New Mexico more than fifty miles back. I think your manhood's safe." She tossed her purse onto floor behind the driver's seat and opened the door before he could come around the car to do it for her. "Why don't you close your eyes and take a nap," she suggested breezily as she adjusted the seat and the rearview mirrors to her shorter stature. "You're going to need your rest for tonight's ride."

He slanted her a wry, wicked look out of the corner of his eye as he folded himself into the passenger seat. "Is that a proposition? So soon?"

"For the *bronc* ride, cowboy." She reached out and tapped the brim of his hat, tipping it down over his face. "Sleep," she ordered sternly, and then spoiled the effect by shooting him a teasing sidelong grin. "The proposition comes later." Her grin widened. "If you're lucky."

"Oh, I've always been lucky." He pulled his hat completely down over his face, crossed his arms over his chest, and leaned back, angling his body into the corner formed by the seat and the car door. "Especially lately," he said from beneath the hat.

Five minutes later, he was sound asleep. He didn't wake up until she slowed down to take the exit ramp to the rodeo arena. As he had that morning, he woke slowly, a muscle at a time. His shoulders rolled under the pale-blue fabric of his shirt. His arms unfolded. His legs shifted. He lifted the hat from his face, ran his other hand through his hair, and resettled the hat.

"We make it on time?" he asked, yawning hugely as he extended his arms straight out in front of him, fingers laced, palms turned outward in a bone-popping stretch.

"You tell me," she said, as she turned the Mustang into the parking lot and began circling, looking for an empty spot among the Volvos, BMWs, and bright shiny sports utility vehicles that dominated. Unlike most rodeos, which drew fans from surrounding ranches and small towns, the Rodeo de Santa Fe was an uptown, upscale affair. The fans were mostly big-city tourists and the artsy locals who'd made Santa Fe a style as well as a place. Beat-up pickups and dusty "ranch" cars were few and far between. Her glossy red rental car fit right in. "The lot's pretty full," she said anxiously. "And I can hear someone singing the national anthem. Does that mean you're too late to compete?"

"Not if I hustle."

"Well, hustle, then. Don't worry about me," she said, when he hesitated. "You go on and do what you have to do. I'll find a parking place, get a ticket and a soft drink, and be in the stands in time to watch you ride. Go on." She waved him away. "Go."

"Yo! Tom! Over here." Tom's bandy-legged traveling partner hailed him as he came out of the rodeo secretary's office with his draw and his competition number in hand. "I didn't think you were gonna make it in time." The man grinned lasciviously. "That little blonde you were with last night looked all lathered up and hot to trot. I'll bet she gave you one helluva ride."

Tom ignored the comment. "Pin this on for me, would you?" he said, and turned around so the other cowboy could pin his number to the back of his shirt.

"Well, come on, pard. Give. Was she as good as she looked?"

His number fastened on, Tom turned around to face

his friend. The other cowboy appeared to be made mostly of barbed wire and bone; he stood a mere five-six with his boots on and weighed a scant hundred and thirty pounds, flak jacket and all. He was a championship-caliber bull rider, currently number eight in the rankings, which put him squarely in contention for the finals in Vegas come December. He and Tom had been friends since they were just a couple of snot-nosed troublemakers on the Second Chance Ranch in Bowie, Texas. For that alone, Tom was willing to cut him some slack.

"You didn't dent my truck, did you, Rooster?"

"'Course not. It's parked over yonder, all safe and sound." He jerked his chin, indicating the direction. "On t'other side of the hay barn where there ain't too many other cars 'cause it's so danged out of the way. So—" He waggled his eyebrows. "How was she? Hotter than a firecracker, I bet." His eyes sparkled with vicarious pleasure. "The kind that rides a cowboy real hard and puts him away wet, I'm thinkin'."

"Keys?"

"Got 'em right here." The wiry little cowboy dug into the front pocket of his jeans. "You're not gonna share any of the juicy details, are you?" he complained as he dropped the keys into Tom's open palm.

"Nope."

"Well, hell," he groused. "I don't know why you're bein' so mean-spirited and close-mouthed about some buckle bunny you picked up at Ed Earl's. It ain't like she's anything special or—" The look in Tom's eyes had him reconsidering. "Or is she?"

ROXANNE FOUND A PARKING place between a gleaming BMW convertible and an equally gleaming Cadillac Escalade SUV. After retrieving her purse from the back seat, she made her way across the tarmac to the ticket booth. The air was brutally hot and dry, despite the lateness of the day. The sky was a bleached-out blue, as if it had faded in the unrelenting glare of the sun. The hillsides surrounding the rodeo grounds were barren and brown, except for the expensive new homes—most of them Spanish-style adobes—nestled among their folds.

The ripe smell of livestock permeated everything, mingling with the scents of popcorn, beer and cotton candy from the concession stands, enlivened by drifting hints of sagebrush and hay, overlaid by the somehow fertile smell of the sun-baked land. It was nothing at all like the cool green smell of Connecticut, or the chalkboard-and-glue smells of her regular daily life in the classroom at St. Catherine's. She took a deep breath, savoring the differences, finding them exciting and exotic even after two weeks of constant exposure.

The singer had long since finished her rendition of "The Star-Spangled Banner" by the time Roxanne had paid her entrance fee and entered the rodeo grounds. As she strolled toward the arena, she could hear the announcer extolling the virtues of cowboys in the upcoming steer-wrestling event. Knowing she had plenty of time before the bronc riders would be competing, she stopped to buy a cowboy hat to protect herself from the sun and help her blend in with the crowd, and then she lingered a little longer, selecting just the right hatband to go with it. The one she chose was bright red, like her boots and tank top, a narrow, braided lariat of leather. The ends dangled down over the edge of her hat brim and were finished with flashing silver beads and fluffy little red feathers that nearly brushed her shoulder. She felt like a sure 'nuff cowgirl with it decorating the crown of her straw cowboy hat as she wandered toward the arena through the labyrinth of concession stands that surrounded it.

Besides the usual food and souvenir stands that could be found at nearly any rodeo, there were miniature clothing boutiques and art galleries meant to appeal to the uptown, upscale patrons that frequented the Santa Fe rodeo. In quick succession, Roxanne found herself plunking down her credit card for a snug little denim vest decorated with silver conchas and leather fringe that fit her like a glove, a pair of soft butterscotch leather chamois pants cut like a pair of jeans, a turquoise and silver lariat necklace, a Western-cut shirt with pearl snaps, and a completely impractical white-eyelet skirt with a ruffled hem that she didn't even try to resist. Her purchases just about busted her vacation budget, but what else was a vacation for, if not overindulgence and mindless extravagance? And, besides, she—or, rather, Roxy—needed the clothes.

The barrel racers were doing their thing by the time she finally made her way to the stands, guiding their quick little cow ponies in figure-eight patterns around barrels set up in the arena, the fringe on their Western-cut shirts and their long hair—most of them had long hair—flying as they raced the clock. Roxanne stood at the base of the bleachers, her purse and a bulging plastic shopping bag looped over her shoulder, a large Dr Pepper clutched in one hand, a glossy rodeo program in the other, shading her eyes as she searched for a seat in the jam-packed arena. Spying one about halfway up and off to the far side, she made her way up the metal steps, sidling past a pseudo cowboy in electric-blue, lizard-skin boots with a cell phone pressed to his ear, past the trio of stylish pseudo cowgirls in beaded buckskin blouses, past an artsy couple in gauzy pastel linens and elaborate turquoise jewelry, to a seat next to the metal rail that separated the stands from the bucking chutes and the staging area just beyond them.

The area was bustling with activity. There were wranglers—people who handled the animals and made sure they were where they needed to be—rodeo bullfighters in their outrageous clown outfits, contestants readying themselves for their individual events. Roxanne had been following the rodeo long enough to know that most cowboys had their own special rituals before an event, just like any other athlete. Some wouldn't ride without a picture of their wife or sweetheart tucked in the breast pocket of their shirt; some always wore the same hat or the same pair of socks; some checked and rechecked their gear; others paced, or sat quietly, staring into space, or praying, or just repeating a special mantra over and over.

Roxanne craned her neck, searching the area for a glimpse of her good-looking dangerous cowboy. The saddle-bronc riding event wasn't for a while yet, but she knew Tom's routine from having surreptitiously watched him for the past two weeks.

First, he would sit down, right in the dirt beside
one of the pens if there was nothing else to sit on—
and, often, there wasn't—lay his saddle in his lap, and
go over it meticulously, inch-by inch, checking the
cinches and webbing for wear or weakness, brushing
off dust, picking off bits of straw, polishing the
smooth leather seat with his bandana until it gleamed.
A bronc rider's saddle was his most precious possession; he carried it from rodeo to rodeo, the only constant on every go-round. The horses were different
each time, the venue constantly changed, but the saddle was always the same. A smart cowboy took good
care of it.

She finally spied him, sitting on a wooden bench
near one of the pens. He'd changed his shirt—that's
why she hadn't seen him at first glance. It was beige
now, instead of the blue she'd expected. The Western
yoke and pocket flaps were outlined in dark brown,
making his shoulders look impossibly wide, his hips
impossibly narrow in contrast. His head was bent over
the saddle, his face shielded from her sight by the
brim of his hat, but she could see his hands, moving
slowly, almost caressingly over the saddle, giving it
the same undivided, single-minded attention he'd
given her when she was under those hard, competent
hands. She gulped audibly, her throat suddenly dry,
her pulse suddenly pounding, her face flushed from
more than the heat of the sun. She took a long noisy
sip of her soft drink in a useless effort to cool off,
and wondered how soon they could steal away and
find a motel room.

6

SATISFIED WITH the saddle's condition, Tom rose from the wooden bench, slung the saddle over the blanket on the top rail of one of the unoccupied pens, and ambled on over to view the action in the arena. The barrel racers had given way to the calf ropers, who would soon give way to the bare bronc riders. And then it would be his turn.

Saddle-bronc riding wasn't the glamour event of the rodeo anymore, not the way it had been back in the early days—bull riding held that spot now, thanks to ESPN—but it was *the* classic rodeo event, the one everybody thought of when they thought of rodeo. Style mattered just as much as staying on, and it took years of practice to do it well, which gave the older, more experienced cowboys the edge. Tom wasn't the top-ranked cowboy in the event, but his score in yesterday's rodeo in Lubbock had pushed him to number eighteen in the rankings, close enough to the magic fifteen to make a place in the finals in Las Vegas a distinct possibility.

He glanced up toward the stands, wondering if *she* would still be with him then. They'd agreed they'd only be together until the end of summer, and the finals were in December, so it wasn't likely. Not that he wanted her to be there, anyway. That would make his life way too complicated because he'd already halfway decided that if he made the finals, he was going to ask Dan Jensen's daughter Jo Beth to come to Las Vegas and watch him compete. Dan was a neighboring rancher, with a nice little spread that ran right alongside the Second Chance, back home in Bowie, Texas. Jo Beth was Dan's only child. She was a nice-looking little gal, sweet-natured and hardworking, knew her way around a barn the way most women knew their way around a dance floor. And she'd had a crush on him since she was sweet sixteen. Not that he'd ever looked her way back then; at twenty-four he hadn't been the least bit interested in sweet little girls. But she was a woman now, "full-growed and haired over" as the saying went, and she was back on her daddy's ranch after four years at Texas A&M with a degree in animal science, and marriage on her mind. Her folks had thrown a big shindig to welcome her home and halfway through his first two-step with her, he'd begun wondering if maybe it wasn't time to start thinking about getting married himself. A man could do a lot worse than to marry a woman like Jo Beth Jensen. Especially when the man in question was a rancher who was retiring from the rodeo circuit and settling down to raise cattle and kids. He had a good start on the cattle, but for the kids he needed a wife. And Jo Beth had been tailor-made for the role.

He hadn't asked her, though. He hadn't even hinted that he was thinking about it. And now he was damned glad he hadn't. It wouldn't have set right with his conscience to be engaged to one woman while he was rolling around on motel beds, tearing up the sheets with a different one. Once the summer was over, that would be the time to get things settled with Jo Beth. In the meantime…

He glanced up at the stands again, looking for a tall blond glass of water in a red tank top but couldn't pick her out of the crowd—until she suddenly stood, a big smile on her face, and waved frantically. He started to lift his arm to wave back when he realized she wasn't looking at him. He turned his head, following her line of sight to the young cowboy who sat perched on the top rail of the arena fence with his boot heels hooked on the rung below. The cowboy touched two fingers to the brim of his hat, returning her wave with a jaunty salute and a gallant dip of his head.

A sharp sliver of something very like jealousy pricked Tom as he recognized the other cowboy.

Clay Madison was an up-and-comer, a good-looking young bull rider who was already making a name on the circuit while still in his first year of professional competition, and giving Rooster a run for his money into the bargain. Despite the hot-pink and black-striped shirt and the elaborately fringed and in-laid chaps, which might suggest otherwise to the un-initiated, he was as tough as nails. He was also pretty enough to have more than his share of buckle bunnies panting after him when the rodeo was over. A few of the bolder ones pursued him shamelessly, to the point of hanging around outside the cowboys' locker room like a bunch of cats in heat, waiting for him to come out so they could pounce.

Tom didn't like to think that Slim might be one of them. He didn't like it at all. He was thinking seriously of marching up into the grandstand to tell her so, in no uncertain terms, when the announcer broadcast the news that the saddle bronc event was next up.

ROXANNE FORGOT ABOUT Clay Madison between one breath and the next, turning her attention toward the bucking chutes as she sank back down in her seat. The announcer was reeling off the lineup, extolling the virtues of each horse and man, waxing poetic about the contests to come. Roxanne was only interested in finding out which horse Tom had drawn. The horse counted for half of a contestant's score. A lackluster performance on the part of the horse could bring the score down no matter how well the cowboy rode. A good bucker, on the other hand, could push the score up into the winning numbers, provided, of course, that the cowboy managed to stay on for the full eight seconds.

Tom had drawn Hot Sauce. The two had been paired up several times before, and Tom was a little bit ahead in the win column. He'd managed to ride her to the horn more times than she'd managed to toss him on his butt in the dirt. She was a good bucker, a worthy opponent, a horse who would do her part to put points on the board.

Roxanne watched, her hands curled around the rolled-up program, as Tom climbed up onto the platform behind the bucking chutes and leaned over the rail to gently place his saddle on the mare's back. Most injuries occurred in the chutes where the narrow confines left little room for maneuvering if a horse panicked and started bucking prematurely. But Hot Sauce stood calmly, as much a pro as the man who was saddling her.

She was already wearing the flank strap, a sheep-skin-lined, beltlike apparatus that fit loosely now, but would be pulled tight when the chute opened, provid-ing added encouragement to buck. The added weight of the saddle didn't seem to concern her in the least. Tom made a small, careful adjustment to the way it sat on her back, then used a long, hooked pole to fish for the cinch hanging down the other side of her bar-rel. He pulled it under her belly, drawing it up her side until he could reach down with his free hand to bring it up the rest of the way. Handing the pole to a waiting wrangler, he leaned into the chute to feed the end of the cinch through the O-ring and tighten it down to secure the saddle. The mare tried to swing her head around to see what was going on as the cinch tightened, but she was restricted by the narrow con-fines of the chute. She kicked out with her back feet to show her displeasure with the situation, and rattled the lower rail. The sound startled her. She whinnied in fear and temper, kicking again, and then tried to rear and lost her balance.

Tom's arm was pinned against the rails as thirteen hundred pounds of horseflesh slammed into the side of the chute. Roxanne's fingers tightened around the rolled-up program, but she managed to stifle the frightened scream that rose to her throat.

"EASY, GIRL," Tom murmured. "Easy." He put his free hand against the mare's neck and pushed gently. "Move over, now. That's a good girl," he crooned as she shifted her weight and freed his arm. He flexed it, checking for broken bones or torn ligaments. It throbbed like a son of a bitch, but was otherwise intact. Fortunately, it was his left arm, so he could still ride. Not that he would have considered doing otherwise, even if it had been his right. He'd have just figured some other way to hang on to the reins. Like with his teeth, maybe.

"You okay?" Rooster said from the other side of the chute. "She get you bad?"

"Nothing an ice pack and a cold Lone Star won't take care of." Tom finished securing the saddle with one good hard yank, patted the mare one last time to let her know he was still there, then slowly eased himself over the top rail and lowered his butt to the saddle, careful not to graze her with his spurs and set her off again.

Hot Sauce, apparently over her little tantrum, didn't so much as flick an ear in his direction.

Tom sat equally still, the reins clutched tightly in his right hand, his left resting lightly on the top rail, his attention now entirely focused on the coming eight seconds that would constitute the entire duration of a successful ride. He ran down a mental checklist—reminding himself to keep his legs stretched high, toes turned out, eyes straight ahead—while he sat there, stock-still, waiting for the moment when everything felt just right. Hot Sauce snorted and shifted beneath him, impatient to begin.

"Ready?" someone said.

Tom lifted his left hand from the railing, letting it curve up over his head, and gave one quick, decisive nod.

The gate swung open.

The flank strap pulled up tight.

Hot Sauce screamed in fury and bolted out of the chute, then jerked to an abrupt halt, head down between her legs, front hooves slamming into the ground with enough force to rattle his teeth as she kicked out with her back feet and tried to toss him off over her head. Tom swung his boots down along the mare's sides with the first buck, letting them snap up to her shoulders as her rear hooves slammed back to earth, then bringing them back down as she bucked again. His butt stayed glued to the saddle, his free hand waved in the air, his body swooped and swayed with the wildly gyrating horse as if they were dancing an intricate pas de deux, rather than fighting for supremacy. When the horn sounded, signaling the end of the ride, he let his left leg swing up and over the mare's neck, and jumped lightly to the ground.

"Man, that was one pretty ride," the announcer enthused. "Probably the prettiest ride I've ever seen."

The judges agreed, awarding him a score of ninety-two out of a possible one hundred.

Tom raised his hat to the crowd as they roared their approval.

ROXANNE WAS ON HER FEET and screaming with the rest of them. She wasn't quite sure whether she was cheering because of his phenomenal score, or because he'd escaped unhurt when Hot Sauce slammed him up against the side of the chute. She suspected it was some giddy combination of both, combined with a healthy dose of lustful feelings for the conquering hero. It might be politically incorrect and unliberated of her, not to mention horribly shallow, but seeing him compete—and win!—had her creaming her jeans. She couldn't wait to get her hands on him and show her admiration and approval in a more direct and satisfying way.

Unable to think of a good reason why she *should* wait, she stuffed her crumpled program into her purse, slung it over her shoulder with her shopping bag, and headed down the steps of the grandstand. There was a guard at the entrance to the livestock area, presumably checking passes, which she didn't have. The old Roxanne would have politely waited outside the fenced-off area until Tom finally appeared. The new Roxy waited until the guard was occupied with someone else, then slipped through the rails and went to find Tom herself.

"Hi, there, sugar," she said, batting her eyes at the first cowboy she saw. "Can you tell me where I might find Tom Steele?"

"He was headed for the locker room, last I saw him." The cowboy motioned toward one of the outbuildings near the main barn. "I'm right here, though. Sure I can't help you, instead?"

"You already have, sugar. Thanks ever so," she

said, mixing a little Marilyn in with the San Antonio barrel racer before she turned and headed toward the cowboys's locker room.

"Hey, Roxy. Roxy! Wait up!"

Roxanne looked around at the sound of her name to see Clay Madison bearing down on her. "Well, hey, good-lookin'," she said by way of greeting, and then narrowed her eyes in mock suspicion. "You followin' me?"

"I thought *you* were following *me*. I decided I might as well make it easy on both of us—" he flashed her a good-natured, good-ol'-boy grin designed to make him look as harmless as a puppy "—and let you catch me."

Roxanne wasn't fooled. She'd seen that John Travolta grin before, up close and personal, and knew the lethal charms it disguised. "Well, sugar, I do appreciate the offer, but I'm afraid I'm going to have to decline. I'm meeting someone."

"Again?"

Roxanne laughed at his hangdog expression. "Tell you what, sugar. You can escort me over there. Just like you did last night." She tucked her hand into the crook of his elbow. "I'm headed for the cowboys' locker room."

"You mind tellin' me who's beatin' my time?" he asked as he fell into step beside her. "Maybe it's someone I can put out of commission."

Roxanne had her doubts about that. "Tom Steele." She slanted a glance up at him out of the corner of her eye. "Think you can take him?"

Clay had his doubts about it, too, but, "Hell, yes!"

he said because that's what she expected. "Would you be mine if I did?"

"Hell, yes," she said, and they both laughed, knowing it was all in fun, knowing they had gotten past whatever attraction might have been between them last night and emerged on the other side of it with nothing more than the potential to be friends.

Tom didn't know it, though.

He exited the cowboys' locker room, hat in hand, just in time to see Roxanne lean in and plant a kiss on Clay Madison's peach-fuzz cheek. That little sliver of something that might have been jealousy grew into a throbbing green monster. He slammed the screen door to the locker room just a little harder than necessary to close it. Both Roxanne and Clay turned their heads toward the sound. And then, before anyone could say a word, Roxanne whooped like a cowboy at a Fourth of July parade, dropped her purse and packages, and launched herself bodily at Tom.

He dropped his hat and caught her, automatically, easily, his hands cupping the curve of her jeans-clad bottom as she wrapped her legs around his waist and wound her arms around his neck. And then her mouth smashed into his, her lips opened hungrily, her tongue came seeking, and the big green monster that had taken hold of him turned a deep, pulsating red. He flexed his fingers against the tight curve of her butt, pressing her more firmly against the rock-hard bulge in his jeans, and kissed her back. He was just about ready to fall to his knees and take her down with him, when she pulled away and smiled into his face.

"God! You were fabulous!" She planted another

one on him. Quick and hard and sweet. "You *are* fabulous!" Another smacking kiss. "That was the prettiest ride I've ever seen. Well—" she grinned, her hot whiskey-colored eyes smiling into his "—the second prettiest. Last night was the prettiest." She hitched herself a little higher against him and put her lips against his ear. "I'm so hot for you right now, I'm practically melting," she whispered.

He practically melted, too, right then and there. Would have, too, if he hadn't suddenly spied Clay Madison over Slim's shoulder, standing there grinning like a skunk eating cabbage. Her very public display of affection—talk about cats in heat, he thought!— had gone a long way toward soothing the green-eyed monster, but the sight of the young bull rider standing there as if he were waiting his turn, brought it roaring right back to the forefront again. He let go of her butt and slid his hands up her sides to her arms, curling his fingers around her biceps to loosen her hold on him.

She let go immediately, unlocking her legs from around his waist and her arms from around his neck. "What?" she said, instantly sensing the change in him. "What is it, sugar?"

"While you're with me, *sugar,* you're a one-man woman." His fingers bit into her biceps. "Or you aren't with me."

She stared at him for a full five seconds, her eyes wide and uncomprehending, her mouth half open, as if she meant to say something but couldn't think what it might be. And, then suddenly, understanding dawned. Her eyes narrowed. Her teeth snapped together. "Just what are you accusing me of?"

Without a word, Tom dropped his hands from her arms and stepped back, jerking his chin toward someone behind her.

Roxanne glanced back over her shoulder. Clay. She'd completely forgotten he was there. "Go away," she said, and turned back to Tom without waiting to see if she'd been obeyed.

The old Roxanne would have waited to make sure he was gone, loathe to make a scene in front of witnesses. Then she would have soothed and explained, wanting only to smooth things over before the situation escalated and feelings got hurt, before anyone yelled. The new, improved Roxy let 'er rip.

"How dare you!" she said, and there was nothing soothing in her tone. There was also nothing of the San Antonio barrel racer in it, either. It was all clipped New England indignation. "How dare you stand there and accuse me of being a promiscuous tramp."

"I never said you were a tramp."

"As good as. *While you're with me...you're a one-man woman. Or you aren't with me.*" She spat his words back at him. "Just who else was I supposed to have been with between now and this afternoon?"

Tom lifted an eyebrow and shifted his gaze to the man standing behind her.

Roxanne didn't even turn around. "And just when was I have supposed to have fucked him?" she demanded, using the most shocking, the most graphic term she could think of. "Hmm? Out in the parking lot, maybe? Under the bleachers of the grandstand during the steer wrestling event? When?''

"I didn't say you fucked him! And keep your voice down, goddammit. Do you want everyone to hear you?"

"I don't care who hears me." She was right in his face now, toe to toe and nose to nose, blood pumping with righteous indignation. "I want to know what— *exactly*—you're accusing me of."

"You kissed him," Tom said, and knew, as he said it, just how ridiculous it sounded.

"I *what?*"

"Kissed him," he mumbled.

"I kissed him? Is that what this is about? I *kissed* him?" She turned to Clay, a look of mock confusion on her face. "Did I kiss you, Clay?"

"Yes, ma'am." Eyes sparkling, he touched his finger to his cheek. "Right here. It was quite a little smacker. Very nice, if I do say so as shouldn't."

"That wasn't a kiss." She reached out and grabbed him by the ears. "*This* is a kiss," she said and pressed her mouth to his.

She gave it all she had—lips, tongue, teeth, and a good deal of squirmy body language. It was a wet, seductive, blockbuster of a kiss. When it was over, she thrust him away from her and whirled back to face Tom.

"Now you have something to be pissed about," she said, and socked him in the stomach as hard as she could. It was a good solid jab, with her body behind it, and it took the wind out of him.

He made a surprised-sounding "Woof," and hunched over.

She smiled evilly, satisfied she'd made her point. "See you around, *sugar*," she said, and then turned away, deliberately, and bent over from the waist, her bottom pointed at him like a dare—or an insult—and scooped her belongings off of the ground.

Without a backward glance, she straightened, regal as an affronted queen, and stalked off with her head held high.

If she had a flag, she thought, she'd be waving it. She felt that high, that triumphant, that strong. She'd raised her voice. She'd created a scene and used vulgar language, and—ohmygod!—she'd actually *hit* another person. She'd said exactly what she wanted to say, exactly when she wanted to say it, and she felt *wonderful*. Almost as good as she had last night in the midst of her fifth—or was it sixth?—glorious orgasm. Or this afternoon on the side of the road, when he'd come apart in her hands.

All in all, she decided, there was a lot to be said for unbridled emotional excess. She should have tried it a *lot* sooner.

Behind her, Tom straightened slowly, one hand still clasped protectively over his stomach, and watched her walk away. Maybe it was best this way. He had Jo Beth to think of, after all. A man shouldn't spend the summer tom-catting around when he was seriously thinking about getting engaged come fall. And there was the season to think about, too. He couldn't keep riding like he had today if he was doing a different kind of riding all night. A body could only take so much.

"Man, that little gal sure packs a hell of a wallop," Clay said, grinning when Tom shifted his gaze to glare at him. "In more ways than one," he added, and tugged at his lower lip. "Be a shame to let her get away."

"Hotter than a firecracker," someone else said, and Tom shifted his gaze farther to find that Rooster had apparently been standing behind the screen door of the cowboys' locker room the whole time and had seen the whole sorry incident. Which meant everyone else was going to hear about it before the day was over because Rooster didn't have a discreet bone in his whole wiry body. "It's going to take a whole heap of grovelin' to get back on her good side," Rooster said.

Disgusted with the both of them, Tom shifted his gaze back to the woman who appeared to be walking out of his life. Her back was ramrod-straight, her hips were swinging, the ridiculous red feathers dangling from her hatband were dancing in the breeze. She didn't hesitate, didn't pause, didn't look back over her shoulder. Tom told himself again it was better this way. He told himself he had no intention of trying to get back on her good side. But he didn't believe it for a minute.

She was a tall cool glass of water with a scalding hot spring inside, and he was one sorry-ass son of a bitch who had a whole heap of groveling to do if he wanted to get back in her bed.

Which he did.

In the worst goddamned way.

"Shit," he said.

7

ROXANNE'S HIGH LASTED through the time it took her to walk across the rodeo grounds and the parking lot to her car. It lasted through the time it took her to drive to the nearest motel and get checked in. It lasted through her leisurely bath and a careful application of fresh makeup and the ritual of getting dressed for the evening—*Take that, Tom Steele,* she thought as she buttoned the snug little denim vest she'd bought over nothing but soft, perfumed skin. It lasted on the drive to the Bare Back Saloon, where all the cowboys hung out after the Rodeo de Santa Fe in the hopes of finding some horizontal action.

It faltered a bit when she stepped inside the smoke-filled honky-tonk and saw Tom leaning up against the bar, talking to a certified, card-carrying buckle bunny, the kind who collected belt buckles as trophies and had perfected the art of gnawing the little red tag off the back pocket of a cowboy's Wrangler while he was still wearing them.

She felt a sharp little jab in what she hoped was only her pride, although it felt uncomfortably close to her heart. Was she really so easily replaceable? Could he share what he'd shared with her last night and this afternoon, did the things he'd done, say the things he'd said, and then blithely go out and find someone else to do them with tonight? And if he could switch partners that easily, damn it, then why was he so incensed when he thought *she* had? What difference could it possibly make to him if it was so easy for him to do the same?

Were men and women really *that* different when it came to sex?

She was about to conclude that, yes, indeed, men were pigs and the San Antonio barrel racer had been right—rodeo cowboys *were* irresponsible sons o' bitches and you *couldn't* trust them—when he looked up suddenly and captured her gaze from across the room. Roxanne abruptly decided that maybe she wouldn't pack up her poor little broken heart and head for home, after all.

He still wanted her.

Badly.

It was all there in his eyes. The burning lust that was twin to her own. The injured male pride. The determination not to be the first to give in. Roxanne felt all her confidence return at that one nakedly yearning, stubbornly male look and decided, then and there, that if Tom Steele wanted her, and she knew now that he did, he could have her. But he was going to have to make the first move. And he was going to have to grovel. And she knew just how to make him do both. Hiding a smug little smile of satisfaction, she lifted her chin and turned away, the ruffled hem of her brand-new, white-eyelet skirt swishing around the tops of her red Sweetheart of the Rodeo cowboy boots, and tapped the closest broad shoulder.

"Dance, cowboy?"

TOM FELT the old green monster rear up again as she melted into the arms of her partner, and deliberately tamped it down. She wasn't really interested in that grinning idiot she was dancing with. She was only doing it tick him off and make him come to heel.

"And I'll be damned if I'll dance to her tune," he muttered, and slugged back a long swallow of the single Lone Star he was allowing himself for medicinal purposes.

The rodeo doctor had given him a cortisone shot and a couple of pain pills to take later if his arm started aching. It hadn't—the cortisone had worked just fine—but he didn't want to complicate matters by adding too much alcohol to the mix, just in case.

"What was that, darlin'?" The physically gifted buckle bunny who'd been trying to engage his interest since he walked in the place pressed her gifts up against his arm and giggled in his ear. "I didn't quite hear what you said, sweetie. The music's kind of loud."

He raised his arm to dislodge her and took another pull on his beer. "I said, nice tune," he said.

"Yes, it is." She giggled again. "Would you like to dance?"

"No."

"Oh. Well." She didn't seem to know what to say to that.

Tom took pity on her—and took the opportunity to get rid of her—by tapping a passing cowboy on the shoulder. "Hey, Rooster, I'd like you to meet— What was your name again, honey?"

"Becky."

"Well, Becky, meet Jim Wills. You can call him Rooster, though. Everybody does. He's a champion bull rider—took first place today in the bull riding event, didn't you, Rooster?—and he's one fine dancer, too."

"First place?" she said, her eyes lighting up as she turned her limpid gaze from Tom to Rooster. "Was that you?"

Rooster stuck his scrawny chest out. "Sure as shootin' was."

"He's got a great big silver buckle to prove it, too," Tom said. "He'll probably let you look at it later if you ask him real nice."

Becky giggled and let Rooster sweep her onto the dance floor. The disparity in their heights put her overgenerous breasts nearly at nose level on Rooster, but neither one of them seemed to mind. Rooster liked women in all their myriad sizes and shapes, and Becky appeared more than satisfied to be dancing with a prize-winning bull rider.

Grinning, Tom lifted his beer bottle to his lips for another sip just as Roxanne two-stepped through his field of vision, smiling up into the face of a grinning young stud who was holding her much too close. Tom barely restrained himself from biting the top off of his beer bottle.

"WHY, that's just *so* interestin', sugar," Roxanne heard herself say, and thought she sounded just like

Scarlett O'Hara on the porch of Tara with the Tarleton twins. "I had no idea ridin' bulls was such a complicated process. I mean—" she batted her eyelashes to distract him from the utter inanity of her conversation "—I knew it was *dangerous* an' all, but I had no idea it was *scientific*. You're so brave. And brilliant, too. A regular scientist. My goodness." She lifted her hand from his shoulder and touched her fingertips to her temple. "It's enough to turn a poor girl's head, sure 'nuff."

Oh, my God, she thought, *now I'm* channeling *Scarlett.* If Tom didn't step in pretty soon and rescue her, she was going to make him eat dirt when he finally did show up.

"You're just a double-edged sword, aren't you, sugar?" she said to the cowboy, who seemed to have no idea that she sounded like a character from one the world's best-known novels. "And you've been ridin' bulls for—how long did you say it was?"

"I started riding calves when I was two," he said, and launched into a long explanation about how his daddy had followed the training apparently laid down by rodeo's all-time greatest bull rider, Ty Murray. It included a regimen of fence walking, unicycle riding and sessions on the bucking machine that lasted into the wee hours.

Thankfully, Roxanne didn't have to say much after that. She just smiled until her jaw ached and silently cursed Tom for the no-good, low-down, good-looking, dangerous cowboy he was.

"WHY DON'T YOU just go get her?"

Tom stopped glaring at Roxanne and her dance partner long enough to turn his head and glare at Clay Madison. The young cowboy was decked out all in black—black hat, black shirt, black denim jeans—in an effort, Tom suspected, to capitalize on his resemblance to the Travolta of the *Urban Cowboy* era. "Mind your own damn business," he snarled.

"You know you want to," Clay said.

"What I *want* is to rearrange your pretty face for you."

"You're welcome to try." Clay seemed unperturbed by the implied threat. "Any place. Any time. We can take it outside right now."

Tom seriously considered it. Smashing anything right now would probably make him feel better. Smashing the face of the man who'd swapped spit with Slim while he stood there and watched would make him feel a whole *lot* better. But it would only be a temporary fix. Besides, Clay wasn't the one who'd been doing the kissing. Regretfully, Tom shook his head. "It wasn't your fault," he said.

"No," Clay agreed. "It wasn't." He took a sip of his beer. "It was yours."

Tom wanted to argue with that. He really did. But the kid was right. It *was* his fault. Slim had only done what she'd done—what she *was* doing—because of what he'd said to her. Tom sighed, and went back to watching her whirl around the dance floor.

She had switched partners and was doing the Schottische with one of the rodeo bullfighters, who was still in his clown get-up. Rumor had it that some of the buckle bunnies had a thing for the bullfighters, but had trouble telling who they were without the makeup and baggy pants. Apparently, this guy wanted to make sure he didn't miss out on any chance for some action. Slim was batting her eyes at him, making him think there was a possibility he might actually get it.

"She isn't even remotely interested in him," Clay said helpfully.

"I know that," Tom snapped. Why the hell wouldn't this guy go away and leave him to stew in peace?

"It's all an act. She's doing it to make you suffer."

"I know that, too."

There was a beat of silence as they both watched her partner spin her in a series of quick, showy twirls. Her ruffled white skirt flared high and wide, exposing the tops of a pair of lacy, white, thigh-high stockings and sleek bare thighs before it fluttered back into place. Both men sighed appreciatively.

"Man, she *really* wants to see you crawl," Clay said.

Tom jerked his gaze away from Roxanne long enough to shoot the young cowboy a half irritated, half admiring glare. "How the hell do you know so much about women? A kid like you?"

Clay shrugged. "I've made a lot of 'em mad." He upended his beer, pouring the last of the brew down his throat, and then set the empty bottle on the bar. "The thing is," he said, as he signaled the bartender for another one, "you know you're going to do it sooner or later—a guy's *always* going to do it sooner or later, if he has feelings for a woman—and the sooner you cowboy up and get it done, the sooner you'll be the one she's dancin' with instead of that clown. You leave it too late, though, and you run the risk of leavin' here alone tonight.'' He picked up his fresh beer and took a long swallow. ''Or else you'll end up watching her walk out of here with someone who ain't so pigheaded and prideful.''

Tom knew the awful truth when he heard it. ''Shit,'' he said.

AFTER THE THIRD skipping turn around the dance floor with the painted cowboy, Roxanne decided she'd waited just about as long as she was going to. If Tom wasn't going to come crawling after her on his own, she was going to have to do something to give him a little added incentive. And that incentive was dressed in black and standing next to him at the bar.

''All this dancin' is making me feel a little light-headed,'' she said to the bullfighter, fanning herself for effect. ''Would you mind awfully if I sat the rest of this one out?''

''Would you like something to drink? A beer? A glass of water?''

''Oh, no, thank you, sugar. I think I'll just go to the ladies' room and run some cold water over my wrists for a few minutes. That should perk me up some. Don't feel like you have to wait for me.'' She patted his arm. ''You just go right on ahead and find yourself another partner. I'll probably be a while.''

On her way to the ladies' room, she just happened to sashay down the length of the bar. She walked on past Tom as if she hadn't seen him, then stopped and turned a brilliant smile on the man standing next to him. "Hey, there, good-lookin," she purred, as if he were the only man in the room.

"Hey, yourself," he said, and grinned at her. "Having fun?"

"Sure am." She put her hand on his chest and leaned in a bit, smiling at him from underneath her lashes. "I'd be having more fun if you'd dance with me," she invited in a breathy little voice.

"Well, now, that's the best offer I've had all night." He reached behind him to set his beer on the bar. "I'd consider it an honor to dance with you."

"No," Tom said.

Roxanne stiffened and turned her head toward him, slowly, as if he were some strange species of bug that had suddenly spoken. "I beg your pardon," she said in her frostiest tones. "Were you speaking to me?"

"You know damned well I'm speaking to you." He reached out and curled his fingers around her forearm, pulling her hand away from Clay's chest. "If you want to dance, dance with me."

"What if I don't want to dance with you?"

"Damn it, Slim, don't push me."

"I wasn't aware that I was even talking to you." She looked down at the hand on her arm, and then back up at him. The look in her eyes was pure temptation. Pure fire. Pure female cussedness at its most contrary. "And if you don't remove your hand from my arm, I'm going to have to ask Clay to remove it for you."

Tom decided he damn well didn't want to wait a minute longer to have her in his arms again. Damn, he liked a woman with sass! "I'm sorry, Slim."

Yes! she thought, mentally doing a little victory dance. "Really?" she said, as if she couldn't care less. "What for?"

"For acting like a jealous fool."

"And?"

"And for yelling at you like I did."

"And?"

"And what?" he said, exasperated. "What else did I do?"

"Well, let's see, now. What else *did* you do? Oh, yes, I remember. You called me a tramp."

"Damn it, don't start that again. I didn't call you a tramp."

"You may not have said the actual word, but that's what you meant."

"I did not call you a tramp," he insisted.

"I'm not going to argue semantics with you. You all but came right out and accused me of having sex with Clay right after I'd had sex with you. In my book, that's calling me a tramp." She looked over at Clay. "What do you think, sugar? Did he call me a tramp?"

"Close to," Clay said diplomatically.

"I did not call you a—" Tom clenched his teeth on the word, clamping down on his temper at the same time. Because she was right. And he knew it. He hadn't actually called her a tramp, but that's what he'd implied. Without any proof, without even a hint of tramplike behavior on her part, he'd let suspicion and ego override good sense. Knowing there was no way out of it, Tom suppressed a sigh and did what he had to do. He groveled.

"I'm sorry," he said. "I'm sorry for yelling at you. I'm sorry for implying that you were a tramp. I'm sorry for acting like a goddamned jealous jackass. I was wrong. And stupid. And—" He groped, searching for another word, any word, that would satisfy her and get him back in her good graces. "I was just flat-out wrong, is all. And I'm sorry."

Roxanne smiled beatifically. "I forgive you."

Tom eyed her suspiciously. "That's it? That's all I had to say? You're not going to make me eat shit?"

"Dirt," she said. "I was thinking of making you eat dirt. And no, I'm not."

He couldn't quite believe that's all there was to it. "Why not?"

"Because when I walked in here tonight and saw you talking to that silicone-enhanced little chippy, I wanted to tear her bleached-blond hair out by the roots."

Tom smiled. "You were jealous." He all but crowed the words.

"When you're with me, sugar, you're a one-woman man. Or you're not with me."

Tom's smile widened into a grin. He slipped an arm around her waist and pulled her close. She melted against him, her hands flat on his chest, her face tilted up like a flower to the sun, her luscious ruby-red lips a kiss away from his.

"So," he said, and his voice wasn't quite steady. "You wanna dance?"

She shook her head, brushing her lips back and forth across his in an almost kiss. "No."

"Drink?"

Another brushing butterfly kiss. "Uh-uh."

"What, then?"

She leaned in that tiny, necessary fraction of an inch and pressed her lips to his. When she finally drew back, a long delicious minute later, she had his lower lip between her teeth. She nipped it lightly before letting go. "I've got us a room down at the Round Up. How 'bout we skip the preliminaries and get right to it?"

THEY DIDN'T MAKE IT to the Round Up Motel. They didn't even make it as far as the car. They were hardly a dozen steps past the front door when Tom pulled her into the dark, concealing shadows at the far side of the building and pressed her up against the unpainted plank wall.

His mouth crashed down on hers, lips open, tongue seeking, teeth nipping and nibbling, his hands on either side of her head to hold her still for his invasion. He didn't come up for air until their lips were red and wet and swollen. Just like certain other parts of their collective anatomy.

"I missed you," he said, and skimmed his mouth down the side of her neck with tender, avaricious hunger. "I know it's only been a couple of hours, but I missed you something fierce."

She tilted her head to give him better access, then sighed when he took it. "I missed you, too."

He smoothed his hands downward, palms open, fingers curved, letting them glide over the curves of her shoulders and arms and breasts. "I've been miserable ever since you walked away from me."

"Me, too." She moaned and arched into his caress, lifting her hands to the backs of his to press them more firmly to her breasts. "Oh, me, too."

"I couldn't do anything but think about you." He flicked open the first button on her denim vest. "About this." He flicked open another button, and then another, and another. "These," he said as he brushed back the sides of the vest and exposed her breasts to the warm night air.

The two ends of the silver lariat necklace she'd purchased that afternoon hung between her breasts, the vivid blue stones dangling on a level with her erect nipples, making her look more naked, more sensual than she would have without the added adornment.

Tom sucked in his breath. "You have the sweetest little breasts," he murmured raggedly, and cupped his hands over them, enveloping them completely, squeezing them together so they plumped up in delicious little mounds of flesh that overflowed his hands and caused the turquoise stones on her necklace to disappear into her cleavage. "Sweet little cupcakes." Slowly he drew his hands away, bringing his fingers together in a pinching motion at the tips of her breasts. "With sweet little cherries on top," he said as he rolled her nipples back and forth between his fingertips.

Roxanne felt everything inside her turn warm and liquid and wanting. She arched her body even more, thrusting her breasts outward, pressing her head back against the rough-hewn wall. "Please," she said.

Tom smiled into the night. "Please what?"

"Touch me."

"I am touching you."

"With your mouth."

"Where?"

"On my breasts. Put your mouth on my breasts."

He bent his head, flicked a nipple with his tongue. "Like that?" he said, knowing he was teasing her, knowing she wanted more.

"Yes. Like that. More."

"More how?" He flicked her nipple again. "Like that? Or like this?" He circled his tongue around the hard, distended little bud, slowly, making it thoroughly wet, then drew back and blew on it.

She shuddered.

"Tell me," he murmured. "Tell me what you want and you'll get it."

She put her hands on either side of his head and tried to draw him closer. "More," she said, her voice low and petulant and rasping, a mere breath of sound.

Gently, he took her wrists in his hands and pushed them down to her sides. "Keep them there," he said, and pressed her palms flat against the wall. "And tell me what you want." He leaned in close for a minute, swaying against her, letting the fabric of his shirt rasp against her sensitive nipples. "You can have anything you want," he crooned. His lips hovered a tantalizing inch above hers. "Anything at all. But you have to ask for it."

"Kiss me," she said.

He did. Thoroughly. Completely.

"Now what?"

"Kiss my breasts."

He scattered a wealth of baby-soft kisses over the upper slopes of both breasts.

"My nipples. Kiss my nipples."

He placed a soft sucking kiss on the tip of each breast.

Roxanne's fingers pressed into the wood beneath her palms.

"Tell me," he murmured again, his voice rough and ragged. She'd lost her cornpone-and-molasses twang again and it drove him nearly crazy to hear her talk dirty in that starched New England accent. He circled his tongue around her nipple, slowly, stopping just short of giving her what he knew she wanted. "Tell me what you want, Slim. Tell me and you'll get it."

"Suck them," she said, and moaned when his mouth closed around the tingling tip of one breast.

He drew it deep, taking as much of her breast as he could into his mouth.

She bit back a whimper as he began to suck, and then let loose a low, aching moan when he cupped his hand around the other breast and began rolling the nipple between his finger and thumb.

"Ohmygodohmygod*ohmygod!*"

Tom lifted his head. "You came, didn't you?"

"Yes."

"Do you want to come again?"

"Yes."

"How? No," he said as she reached for his hand, "put your hands back on the wall and tell me. That's the only way you're going to get what you want."

Quivering, aching, feeling thwarted and rebellious

and all the more aroused because of it, she did as he ordered and pressed her palms flat against the wall.

"Good girl." He kissed her approvingly. "Now. Tell me what you want."

"Put your hand between my legs. No. No, under my skirt. Inside my panties. Rub me. Yes, like that. Please. Oh, yes. Yes. Just like that. Right there. Oh. Oh. Oh, please. Oh, Tom. Please, Tom."

"Hands against the wall," he ordered, stopping the tantalizing manipulations of his fingers when she clutched his arms. "And keep your hips still."

Shooting him a fulminating glare, she slapped her palms against the wall and went rigid, biting down her bottom lip in an effort to stay that way.

He rewarded her with the soft, slow strumming of his thumb against her clitoris, just the way he knew she liked it, drawing it out, waiting…waiting… waiting until she was on the screaming edge before he slipped two long fingers inside of her and stroked her G-spot. Her body convulsed as a torrent of feeling burst inside her, her whole body clamping down in an orgy of wild, intemperate, unstoppable sensation.

"Again?" he said, when she'd caught her breath.

"Yes." The word was nearly a sob. "Yes. But I want your cock in me this time," she said, telling him before he could ask. "And I want to touch you."

"Be my guest," he invited, angling his hips so she could get at the fly of his jeans.

She flicked open the metal button on the waistband, then grabbed the two sides and pulled, popping the rest of the buttons in a single motion. His erection bulged through the opening, covered now only by the white knit fabric of his briefs. She grabbed the elastic waistband with both hands and pulled it down. His erection sprang free, iron-hard and pointing straight up at his navel. She trailed her fingertips up its length and then down again, slowly, watching it jerk in response.

Roxanne all but licked her lips in anticipation. "I want this inside me."

"Lift up your skirt," he ordered.

Her gaze on his face, she gathered the eyelet fabric in her fists and pulled it up, slowly, revealing the tops of her red boots and the lacy white stockings. The stocking tops stopped midway between her knees and crotch, held up with lacy elastic bands that gently hugged her thighs. Above them her legs were smooth and bare all the way to the high-cut legs of her white lace panties.

His eyes glazed over, his gaze riveted on the tiny triangle of white lace between her thighs. "Take them off," he said, indicating the panties with a jerk of his chin.

Transferring the froth of fabric to one hand, she attempted to remove the panties one-handed.

Evidently, she was taking too long. "Let me help." He curled his fingers over the waistband, and yanked.

Hard.

The fragile lace split without a protest.

Roxanne nearly came again, right then and there.

Tom grabbed her hips in his hands, curling his fingers under her bare bottom, pulling her forward and lifting her all in one smooth motion.

She started to come again as soon as he entered her.

"Not yet. Not yet," he murmured desperately, pressing her hips hard against the wall to keep them both from coming.

It was too late for Roxanne. She went up and over, her face buried in the curve of his neck to muffle the sounds of ecstasy.

Tom managed to hang on, holding back until her spasms subsided, and they could begin again, together. And then he began moving. Slowly. Powerfully. Pumping in and out of her in unconscious time to the heavy beat of the music pulsating against the wall at her back. The band was playing "Wild Thing," the unlikely hard-rock anthem of the rodeo cowboy. The crowd was really into it, stamping and screaming, rattling the walls of the old barnlike building from the inside, while they shook it from the outside to the same wildly sensual beat.

Wild thing, I think I love you!

Oh, no, Roxanne thought, as she tumbled over the edge again into the mindless abyss of blinding physical sensation.

Did she?

8

ROXANNE TURNED IN her Mustang at the Santa Fe airport on the theory that there was no reason to waste money on a rental when they'd be driving to the same places all the time.

"If you get sick of us, you can always rent yourself another car and be on your way," Rooster said as they all settled into the cab of Tom's pickup for the one-hour drive from Santa Fe to Albuquerque.

It was one of the extended crew cab models, big and black and macho, so there was plenty of room for the three of them as well as the occasional fourth passenger—or even a fifth, if nobody minded getting cozy and they ran across a cowboy in need of a lift to the next rodeo. The truck bed was fitted with a low, windowless camper top that could be locked to secure their gear. It was equipped with an inflatable mat and a double sleeping bag, so it was even possible to sleep in shifts, if not actual comfort, during the frequent overnight hauls between venues. Given that it was the virtual home-away-from-home for two men, Roxanne found the interior of the truck was surprisingly neat and tidy. There was a big cooler behind the driver's seat for soft drinks and cold cuts, and a plastic bag for the inevitable trash one accumulated on a long road trip. There was a thick stack of well-worn maps stuck under an elastic band on the visor, a jumble of mostly country-western CDs mixed in with several books-on-tape in a shoebox on the floor, a radar detector mounted under the dashboard, and nearly a dozen paperbacks and as many magazines strewn over the top of it.

Someone, Roxanne noted, was quite fond of the more sensational tabloid magazines, which, together with the books, made for a very eclectic mix of literature. There was a copy of the most recent *Prorodeo Sports News,* of course, three or four of the requisite Louis L'Amour and Zane Grey westerns, a couple of Robert Parker and Sue Grafton detective stories, a Tony Hillerman, a meaty Wilbur Smith novel, a recent Oprah pick, and—

"Harry Potter?" she said, picking up the young magician's latest adventure.

"That's Tom's," Rooster pointed out quickly, in case anyone thought he might be reading a kid's book.

"I like to keep up with what my students are reading," Tom said. "Turns out, it's a real good book. Have you read it?"

Roxanne goggled, just a bit. "'Students?'"

"Tom's a teacher," Rooster said helpfully. "When he's not rodeoin' he spends most of his time trying to pound some learnin' into the young hooligans at the Second Chance Ranch."

Roxanne really did goggle then. She couldn't help it. Her good-looking, dangerous cowboy was a *teacher?*

"Surprise," he said softly.

IT WAS NEARLY an eight-hour drive from Albuquerque to Phoenix, if you kept to the speed limit. It was considerably less if you pushed it. After only two days in their company, Roxanne had already learned that cowboys *always* pushed it. Even cowboys who taught school. It was simply the nature of the beast, and the way the rodeo game was played if you wanted to win.

A cowboy had to compete at a lot of rodeos to make a living. And a lot of rodeos meant a lot of traveling.

"Say you win first place at one of the big venues and pull down fifteen hundred, maybe two thousand dollars for a single event," Tom said quietly, talking mostly to keep himself awake on the long overnight haul. "That's considered big money because, more often, you're looking at a couple of hundred dollars, max. But say you win that two thousand. You've got to pay your entry fees out of that, and those can be four or five hundred dollars at a top venue. You've got to pay all your own traveling expenses. If you're a family man, with a wife and kids waiting for you at home, you've likely got expenses there, too. A cowboy can be a top rodeo star and still make less than a hundred thousand a year, gross. Usually way less."

She wanted to ask what he'd "pulled down" for the third place he'd taken in the saddle bronc event that afternoon, but didn't. It wasn't any of her business what he made or didn't make. "Then why do you do it? Why does anybody do it?"

"Why did Joe Namath play football with braces on both knees? Or Steve Young keep playing after his sixth concussion? Sure as hell, neither one of them needed the money."

"So you're telling me it's the love of the game? That you actually *like* being tossed on your head at regular intervals?"

"Hey, now, no need to be insulting," he chided. "I don't get tossed my head on a regular basis. Just often enough to keep it interesting for the paying customers."

"But to risk life and limb for that piddley amount of money! That's just crazy, is what it is."

"No, darlin'," he drawled, "that's rodeo."

"HERE, ROXY, take a sip of my Co'-Cola," Rooster said, thrusting the familiar red-and-white can at her when she paused to clear her throat. "Wet your whistle. We can't have you gettin' dry, now, can we?"

Roxanne took the can from him and took a small sip. It was the full-octane version of the soft drink, chock-full of caffeine and sugar, too sweet for her taste and warm, to boot, from being clenched between Rooster's hands. But she'd been reading out loud for the past two hours and needed, as he'd said, something to wet her whistle. Having done so, she handed it back to him with a smile, silently vowing to make sure they added diet cola and a six-pack of spring water to the contents of the cooler in the back seat at the next refueling stop.

"For a kid's story, that Harry Potter ain't half bad," Rooster said, and gave Tom a friendly whack on the back of the head. "You shoulda told me how good it is. I might have started in to read it myself if I'd known.''

"I did tell you." Tom said without rancor, neglecting to add that it hadn't done any good because Rooster had never willingly cracked a book in his life.

His choice of reading material tended toward the tabloids, *People,* the latest issue of the *Prorodeo Sports News,* and, once a year, the swimsuit issue of *Sports Illustrated.* Like most cowboys, he did love a good yarn, though, and was an avid fan of the books on tape that could be rented at one truck stop and returned down the road at another. It hadn't taken him long to discover that having somebody read to him was better still for whiling away the long, dreary hours on the road.

"It is a good story, isn't it?" Roxanne said, turning her head to smile at Rooster over her shoulder.

Tom cast a speculative sideways glance at her, amazed at her patience and good humor, not to mention her skill at reading out loud. Not everyone could do it well, either reading too fast or too slow, or plodding along in a monotone that could render a book boring no matter how talented the writer. She read with verve and animation, bringing the characters to life in a way that suggested she'd had a lot of practice—and making Tom wonder just where she'd acquired the skill.

"You need another sip, Roxy?" Rooster said, none too subtly prodding her to resume reading. "You want me to open you up a cold one so's you can finish the next chapter?"

"No, thanks," she said and, taking the hint, resumed regaling them with the magical adventures of Harry Potter and his friends.

"THERE'S A RODEO someplace in the country almost every day of the year," Tom told her as they sped along the highway between Phoenix and Window Rock, which was seven and a half hours away in the heart of the Navajo reservation in Arizona. "Considerably more, of course, during the summer months," he continued, his voice low to avoid waking Rooster, who slept stretched out on the back seat of the cab because sleeping in the back, inside the camper top, made him carsick. "On weekends, it's not unusual for a cowboy to compete in three or four different rodeos in as many different cities. Two a day, sometimes, if he can squeeze them in. Fourth of July week is especially crazy because of all the festivals and celebrations going on then. A lot of them have rodeos attached."

Roxanne tried, unsuccessfully, to stifle a yawn. "Why?"

Tom slanted her a glance out of the corner of his eye. "Why what?"

"Why would you want to compete in more than one rodeo a day?"

"Points," said Rooster from the back seat, proving he wasn't asleep, after all.

Roxanne started and looked around guiltily, devoutly hoping he'd been asleep thirty minutes ago when she'd distracted Tom from the tedium of the road with a little digital sex.

"Points and money," Rooster said. "Each dollar

you earn in winnings counts as a point in the stand-ings. And only the top fifteen cowboys—the top fif-teen money winners—in each event go to the finals in Las Vegas. The more rodeos you enter, the more money you earn, the more points you win. See?''

''That's the theory, anyway,'' Tom said.

''So, how many rodeos does a cowboy have to en-ter to get the points he needs to make the finals?'' Roxanne asked.

''Well, now, that all depends. You ride in a lot of little Podunk rodeos, with Podunk purses, you don't make many points. What you gotta do is hit as many of the big venues as you can, that's where the big money is.''

''Big being a relative term,'' Tom said dryly.

Rooster paid no attention. ''Cities like Dallas and Fort Worth. Denver. Phoenix. That's where the big money is. And your big state fairs and festivals, now, there's good money to be had there, too. The Buffalo Bill Rodeo in North Platte. Pike's Peak or Bust in Colorado Springs. Frontier Days in Cheyenne. And Mesquite, a'course. The Mesquite rodeo has become real popular. There's a rodeo going on there purt' near every weekend. Big money there.''

''Big being a relative term,'' Roxanne said, and earned a sly, sidelong grin from the driver.

''No, ABSOLUTELY NOT. No way.'' Roxanne slapped at Tom's hands and tried to stifle an excited giggle. ''I am absolutely *not* going to have sex in the back of a pickup,'' she said primly, even though the very thought of it had her juices flowing. "They'll hear us."

"They" were Rooster and two other cowboys who were hitching a ride to the next rodeo. Their car had overheated in the middle of the Arizona desert, causing the engine to freeze up. Since it was on its last legs, anyway, an oil-guzzling junker purchased for a couple of hundred dollars, they simply left it where it was, hefted their gear on their backs, and started walking. Tom picked them up about a hundred miles east of Window Rock, which worked out just fine because it gave them two more drivers on the long haul to Canon City.

"Nobody's going to hear a thing, Slim," Tom wheedled, his voice warm and cajoling. "Rooster's got his George Strait CD turned up full blast. And even if he didn't, what with the road noise and the wind, and us back here all private and cozy under the camper, snug as two bugs in a rug, they wouldn't hear us, anyway. Not unless you scream real loud." He grinned wickedly, and tugged at the placket of the Western-cut shirt she'd bought at the rodeo in Santa Fe, popping the little pearl snaps to expose her leopard-print push-up bra to his avid gaze. "Damn, you wore this on purpose, didn't you?" He ran his hand over her décolletage, tracing the upper curves of her plumped-up breasts with his fingertips. "You know it makes me crazy."

"No," she said, although it was true. "I wore it because it's the last clean one in my suitcase until we can stop at a Laundromat."

He skimmed his hand down over her stomach to

the top button on her jeans and popped it open, too. "Are you wearin' those sexy little leopard panties, too?" He pulled the zipper down before she could stop him. "Let me see."

She slapped his hand away again. "I mean it. We're not having sex back here."

He traced a fingertip along the edge of her panties. "How about we just fool around a little bit, then?"

"Absolutely not," she said, and rolled over on her side, away from him. "Go to sleep. You've got to ride in less than eight hours."

"I'd rather ride you right now," he murmured, and kissed her nape.

Roxanne steeled herself against temptation. "Sleep," she said sternly, and closed her own eyes.

"I'm too keyed up to sleep." He slid his hand over her hip and down inside the opened fly of her jeans. His palm was flat on her belly, his long, callused fingers sliding under the edge of her panties to touch the crinkly blond hair that covered her mound. He brushed them back and forth, just above where she was beginning to crave his touch. "I'd probably drop right off to sleep if I was more relaxed."

"Relax yourself," she suggested. But she scooted back, just a little, until the curve of her butt was pressing into his groin and he didn't have to reach quite so far to caress her.

He returned the pressure of her hips, snugging his erection up against her, and inched his fingers a little further down inside her panties. "Didn't your mother ever tell you that relaxing yourself will make you go blind?"

"My mother didn't talk to me about relaxation. She talked about the importance of a diversified stock portfolio and how to hire a good caterer and cleaning ser—" She gasped as his fingers found just exactly the right spot. The gasp turned to a moan, and her hips rolled, moving rhythmically against his clever fingers.

He took advantage of her momentary distraction to ease her loosened jeans down over the curve of her hip, baring her to mid-thigh. His fingers slid deeper between her legs, cupping her, his long index finger sliding in and out of her wet sheath, his thumb riding her clitoris.

She bit back a shriek. "Stop that," she moaned, casting an apprehensive glance toward the cab of the truck.

He started to draw his hand away.

She grabbed at it, keeping it right where it was. "No, don't!"

He chuckled wickedly and popped the buttons on his own fly, freeing his erection. Roxanne arched her back and wriggled her butt against him, her legs parting as far as the restricting jeans would allow. Tom slipped his cock into her from behind and began a slow, leisurely pumping, while his fingers continued manipulating her clitoris from the front.

"Don't scream, now," he whispered, just as she was about to come. "They might hear you."

THEY CHANGED PLACES at the halfway point, the two hitchhiking cowboys stretching out in the back of the truck to catch a little shut-eye, while Tom and Rox-

anne shifted to the front seat. Rooster, as usual, unfolded himself along the back seat to sleep, unable to
stomach the close confines of the camper top. They
rolled into Canon City, Colorado, just in time for the
afternoon rodeo. Barely.

Tom took first place on the back of a high-rolling
bronc named White Lightning, which was enough to
nudge him one step up in the standings. Rooster
pulled down second, squeezed out of first by the extra
two points won by Clay Madison. They packed up as
soon as their events were over, pushing hard to make
the two and a half hour drive to Elizabeth in time for
the evening performance.

Tom drew a respectable ride in his second rodeo of
the day, pulling down third on a dun-colored pile
driver that hit the ground stiff-legged, snapping Tom's
teeth together and sending a jolt up his spine with
each buck. Rooster drew the Widow Maker. The animal was a particularly bad-tempered two thousand
pound Brahman with a reputation for going after
downed cowboys. He was dangerous in the chutes,
too, and had been known to rear up and fall over
backward on top of the cowboys who tried to ride
him. If a cowboy could stick, he'd be sure to pull
down a top score. But not many had been able to
stick. In the three years the Widow Maker had been
on the circuit, two cowboys had died from the injuries
he'd inflicted. Countless others wore scars inflicted by
his hooves and horns.

Knowing all this, Roxanne paled when she heard
the name of the bull Rooster had drawn. Rooster
rubbed his hands together and cackled with glee; a

ride to the horn on the Widow Maker would earn him a guaranteed first place, and put him ahead of Clay Madison. The crowd roared and stamped their approval when the pairing was announced over the loudspeaker, anticipating a good show in their favorite event.

Bull riding was the most popular event at the rodeo because—in Roxanne's opinion, anyway—it was the bloodiest, most dangerous event, with the most potential for the "wrecks" so beloved by the fans and the camera crews from ESPN and the Nashville Network. As a general rule, it drew the smallest, most compact cowboys as competitors. The late great Lane Frost, who'd been killed by a bull named Taking Care of Business, hadn't been much bigger than a jockey. Ty Murray, the All-Around Cowboy for three years running, was only five feet six inches tall—and that was only, some said, if you measured him with his boots on.

"It all has to do with gravity," Rooster explained earnestly as Roxanne pinned his number on his back and tried to pretend she wasn't the least bit concerned about his safety during the upcoming ride. "A man's center of gravity is in his chest, see? And the closer the center of gravity is to the bull, the easier it is to stay on. That's why you ain't gonna see any six-footers like Tom at the bull ridin' finals. Gravity will do 'em in every time."

It was gravity that did Rooster in at the Elizabeth rodeo. Gravity and a bull named Widow Maker. The animal came out of the chute like a rocket shot off the launching pad at NASA. Its massive body rose straight into the air, twisting as it toppled the cowboy on its back into the dust and rolled over on him.

Roxanne surged to her feet with the rest of the crowd, her hands pressed to her mouth to stifle the scream that rose to her lips. Paralyzed, unable to move, she watched the bullfighters rush in, standing between the downed cowboy and the enraged bull, distracting him before he could do any more damage, driving him out of the arena and into the pens behind it. And then Tom was vaulting over the fence from behind the chutes, beating the paramedics to his fallen friend. Roxanne shook off the paralysis that gripped her and raced down the grandstand steps, fighting her way through the milling crowd, ignoring the shout of the security guard as she ran through the gate that led to the staging area.

Rooster was laid out on an examining table in the medical tent when she got there, his eyes closed, his lips white and compressed, his fingers clutching the rounded edges of the table in a white-knuckled grip while the medics worked over him. His flak jacket had already been removed and lay in a crumpled heap on the floor. The right leg of his chaps had been unbuckled and folded back, the leg of his jeans split and torn open to mid-thigh. One medic poked and prodded his exposed leg, while another took care of checking vital signs. Roxanne approached the head of the table, out of the way of the medical personnel, and reached out, touching Rooster's white, drawn face with a gentle hand.

''Rooster?''

His eyes fluttered open. ''Hey, Roxy.'' He managed

a smile for her. "Tom," he said, looking up at the man who stood behind her. "How bad is it, pard?"

"Not too bad," Tom said. "Doesn't look like anything's broken." He glanced at the medic poking at Rooster's leg for confirmation.

"Nope, nothing broken," the medic said cheerfully. "Nothing bleeding, either, 'cept for a few scrapes. The knee's already swelled up like a balloon though, and it's gonna be badly bruised. Could be just a sprain." He shrugged. "Could be torn ligaments. I can't say for sure without X rays. You're gonna have to take him over to the hospital in town to find that out."

"No hospital," said Rooster. "No time. I gotta ride tomorrow in Fort Collins."

"Rooster!" Roxanne was appalled. "You have to go to the hospital. That bull rolled right over on top of you. All two thousand pounds of him. You might have internal bleeding."

The medic who'd been checking vital signs looked up at that. "Doubt it," he said as he released the blood pressure cuff from around Rooster's arm. "Pressure's normal. If he was bleeding inside it'd be way down."

"There's still his knee," Roxanne insisted. "He needs to get it X-rayed."

"I ain't goin' to no hospital, so just get that thought right out of your head." Rooster struggled to sit up, shifting to swing his legs over the side of the table. His face paled a bit and the breath hissed out from between his teeth but he managed to stay upright without swaying. "Hell, this ain't nothin'. I just twisted the damned thing, is all. I've done worse trippin' over my own feet on the dance floor. 'Sides, there ain't a bull rider in the world who don't have bad knees. It comes with the territory. Just slap some ice on it,'' he said to the medic, ''and give me a coupl'a pain pills and I'll be good as new.''

''Good as new! You can't even stand up.'' Roxanne parked herself in front of him, preventing him from doing just that, and jammed her hands on her hips. ''With the condition that knee's in, I doubt you could even crawl.'' Her voice rose with her agitation, her New England accent becoming crisper and sharper with each syllable. ''So just how the *hell* do you think you're going to be in any condition to ride tomorrow?''

Rooster grinned. ''Hotter than a firecracker,'' he said admiringly.

Roxanne folded her arms across her chest, refusing to be charmed.

Rooster sighed. ''I don't hafta walk to be able to ride, Roxy.'' He looked to the man standing behind her for confirmation. ''Tell her, Tom.''

Roxanne whirled around. ''Yes, tell him, Tom,'' she said. ''Make him go to the hospital.''

''Rooster knows what he's doing,'' Tom said. ''If he says he doesn't need to go to the hospital, he doesn't need to go. And I'm not about to try and make him.''

''Oh, for crying out loud! What is it with you guys?'' Roxanne's fulminating glare took in not only Rooster and Tom, but all the other battered and bruised cowboys being tended to in the medical tent. ''It's that stupid cowboy tradition, isn't it? It wouldn't be manly to admit you're hurt, would it? No, of course not! You could have six bleeding wounds, two broken ankles and a concussion, but you'd still have to suck it in and cowboy up, just to prove you have real try. God forbid, any of you should admit you're hurt or in pain. The world as we know it might come to an end.''

"Tom rode once with a broken collarbone,'' Rooster said when she paused for breath. "At the Mesquite Rodeo, wasn't it, Tom?''

Tom nodded.

"Did you have a concussion that day, too? Or was it just the collarbone?''

"Just the collarbone,'' Tom said, his lips quirking up at the outraged expression on Roxanne's face. "The concussion was at the Bowie Rodeo a year ago last May.''

"That's right, I remember now.'' Rooster nodded. "It was just the collarbone that day in Mesquite,'' he said to Roxanne. "He had to have the bone reset after the last go-round, but it sure was a pretty ride.''

"Idiots!'' She threw her hands up in exasperation. "You're all idiots. Morons. I wash my hands of you. You can all kill yourselves for all I care,'' she said, and stomped out of the medical tent with the cowboys' delighted laughter following behind her.

SHE DIDN'T WASH HER HANDS of them, though. Instead, she read the final chapters of Harry Potter to them by flashlight, keeping Tom awake during the long nighttime drive to Fort Collins, keeping Rooster's mind off the throbbing pain in his knee. The next day at the rodeo arena, when his knee had turned ten shades of purple and swollen to the size of a cantaloupe, despite the constant icing, she was right there at his side, offering pain pills and sympathy, ready to help him hobble over to the chutes if that's what he wanted.

It was Tom who convinced him to turn out. "You drew a piss-poor bull, anyway, a real dink, so you probably wouldn't place no matter how good you rode," he said. "And, hell, any cowboy who's ranked in the top ten can afford to take one goddamned day off to rest up."

Rooster insisted on riding in Casper, though. There was good money to be had there, and he'd drawn a decent ride. And young Clay Madison was steadily advancing in the ranks behind him.

During the long frantic Fourth of July weekend, they did Riverton and Hot Springs, Worland and Cody, Billings and Bighorn, and half a dozen other small towns in quick succession, three rodeos a day sometimes, when scheduling and distance made it possible. Somewhere along the way, Roxanne took over the domestic duties for what had become their little family. Mostly out of self-defense against widening thighs and clogged arteries.

"I refuse to eat another greasy hamburger at another greasy truck stop," she said, her arms folded over her chest in a way that her traveling companions knew meant she'd come to the end of her rope—and theirs. "From now on, we eat normal food, like normal people. Vegetables," she elaborated, when they just looked at her. "Fresh fruit. Salads. Whole-wheat bread."

"I had a salad last night with my dinner," Tom said, just to aggravate her. "Vegetables, too."

"Wilted iceberg lettuce with gloppy pink dressing is not a salad." She sniffed disdainfully. "And canned green beans cooked in bacon grease do not qualify as a vegetable in my book."

She took the truck the next day while they were competing and found a Wal-Mart. When it was time to stop for dinner, she demanded they bypass the easy-off, easy-on, fast-food joints and truck stops, directing them, instead, to pull over at the next rest area.

"There's a camp stove in the back of the truck," she said, wrapping the sleeves of one of Tom's shirts around her waist like an apron to protect her last clean pair of pants.

She'd been reduced to wearing a pair of her pre-Roxy khaki slacks. They were conservatively cut, of course, with a pleated front and a cuffed hem. Paired with one of her snug little tank tops and her red boots, with a bandana threaded through the belt loops instead of her shiny alligator belt with the gold buckle, she thought she'd achieved a sort of funky urban-cowgirl-meets-Connecticut-Yankee kind of chic. At least, nobody'd laughed when they'd seen her coming.

"The propane tank is in the back seat next to the cooler," she continued, ordering them to fetch and carry as easily as she did her students. "Utensils and paper plates are in the bag with the groceries. By the time you've washed up, I'll have some veggie sticks ready for you to munch on."

A half an hour later they were dining on skinless, boneless grilled chicken breasts, a green salad with fat-free dressing, and whole-wheat rolls. Rooster grumbled and rolled his eyes when she put the grilled chicken in front of him—"I generally like my chicken fried," he said—but he ate every morsel and asked for seconds.

"Since you were such good boys and cleaned your plates—" she pulled another container out of her magic bag of foodstuffs "—you get dessert." She placed an aluminum tray of frosted brownies between them on the picnic table. "I stopped at a bakery on the way back from the Wal-Mart," she said, delighted with their reaction to her surprise.

It was later, as they were loading the camp stove and supplies back into the truck that she mentioned the laundry. "I didn't get a chance to stop by a Laundromat today. But I will tomorrow while you're competing. If you'll give me your things, I'll wash them at the same time I do mine."

"You want my skivvies?" Rooster said, scandalized.

It was Roxanne's turn to roll her eyes. "I've seen men's underwear before, Rooster. I've got three brothers."

"Yeah, well, you ain't seen mine before."

She put her hands on her hips. "You aren't going to have time to do any of your own laundry in the foreseeable future," she said. "And if you don't do any laundry, then you'll have to wear what you've been wearing for the last two days. And if that happens, you're riding in the back of the truck until you do have time to do it because you're already beginning to smell like one of those bulls you ride.'' She smiled sweetly. "But it's up to you, of course.''

Tom, who wasn't shy about his skivvies and knew a good thing when he saw it, handed over his dirty laundry without a fuss.

THEY STAYED AT A MOTEL after the last rodeo of the weekend in Miles City to ensure a full night's sleep before tackling the nine-hour drive to the one billed as the *Daddy of 'em All*—Frontier Days in Cheyenne, Wyoming.

Amazingly enough, cowboys considered the *Daddy of 'em All* to be a vacation of sorts. The event lasted for ten days, with a rodeo in the same fairground arena every day. As there was no traveling from venue to venue, the cowboys got to bed down in the same place for a while, be it in a motel or a camper parked on the fairgrounds, and eat food that didn't come from a greasy-spoon truck stop. Those who had families they rarely saw could have them come to Cheyenne and be assured they'd have long stretches of uninterrupted time to spend together between the eight-second rides. There was top-name country-western entertainment nearly every day after the rodeo, and all the usual fairground attractions, plus Indian Dancing exhibitions, art shows and a special performance by the United States Air Force Thunderbirds.

"It makes," Tom said, "for a real party atmosphere."

It also had the largest purse in professional rodeo.

A cowboy who'd slipped behind in the standings could make it all up—and then some—in Cheyenne.

None of that mattered to Roxanne, though, as she snuggled down into the crisp, cool sheets of a Motel 6 with a blissful sigh. She'd had a long, leisurely bath, and a real dinner in a real restaurant with real linens on the table and fresh salads on the menu and a decent wine list, and now she was faced with the utterly delicious prospect of a full night's sleep in an unmoving bed—for the second night in a row!—before she had to be up to face the craziness of the Frontier Days celebration.

She could hear Tom rummaging around in the bathroom—showering, shaving, gargling—and then the door opened and he strolled out with one of the too small motel towels wrapped around his lean hips. His body was long and lanky, without an excess ounce of fat anywhere. Wide shoulders. Broad chest. Washboard stomach. Tight little cowboy butt. Strong horseman's thighs. A perfect masculine specimen, marred only by the scars of his profession. He'd been stepped on, kicked, punched, battered, bitten and broken, and nearly every part of his body showed silent evidence of it.

There was a crescent-shaped scar on his right tricep where an angry horse had taken a bite out of him, and another one just under his bottom lip where his own teeth had snapped together during a particularly bone-jarring ride. He had a steel pin in his right thigh and a knee that talked to him when the weather changed. Both of his shoulders had been dislocated at least twice, his collarbone had been broken once—at the rodeo in Mesquite—and he'd lost count of all the dislocated fingers, crushed toes, and torn ligaments he'd racked up over the years. And, then, of course, there were the fading yellowish-green bruises that still ran down the length of his left arm, courtesy of a feisty little mare called Hot Sauce. Although he claimed it was fine and didn't bother him at all, he often rubbed it absently, just above his elbow where the bruises had been the worst.

"Tell me again why you do it," Roxanne said as he dropped the towel and crawled into bed beside her.

"Do what?" He wrapped his arms around her, pulling her close, and bent his head to kiss her.

She put a fingertip to his lips, stopping him. "This," she said, tracing the faint white scar under his lip. "And this." She touched the bump on his collarbone where the bones had knit imperfectly. "And this." She ran her hand down the mottled bruises on his arm. "What makes you risk life and limb, over and over again?"

"The sheer glory of being a cowboy," he said without missing a beat.

"No. I'm serious."

"So am I."

"Where's the glory in living like a nomad? Of driving three hundred miles or more every day, just so you can spend eight seconds on the back of some half-wild animal? The pay's lousy, the food's worse—"

"Food's been pretty good lately," he reminded her. "Thanks to you."

"—and the benefits are nonexistent," she said, ignoring the interruption.

"So, I guess the magic's worn off for you, huh?" His tone was teasing, but the look in his eyes was suddenly guarded and wary. "Does that mean you're going to be packing up and heading back to whatever New England state it is you came from?"

"Connecticut," she said. "And, no, it doesn't mean I'm packing up. The magic of the rodeo may have faded—" she cupped his lean cheeks between her hands and smiled up into his face "—but your magic just keeps getting stronger and stronger."

To her delight, he very nearly blushed.

"I intend to hold you to our agreement, Tom Steele. I'm a one-man woman—and vice versa—until the end of the summer."

Which was only six short weeks away.

Roxanne felt a stinging in her eyes at the thought, and a painful tightening in her chest. She blinked once, hard, and willed the feeling away.

They still had six weeks, and she intended to make the most of them.

"But I still want to know why you do it," she said.

"We'll talk about it later," he murmured, and bent his head to take her lips. "Much later."

She sighed and let the magic take her as his lips covered hers. It was a leisurely kiss, soft and sweet and deliciously unhurried. Their lovemaking had always been tempestuous before, frenzied and wild. Now it was indescribably tender.

He took a long time kissing her. Her lips, her cheeks, her eyelids and temples, the soft curving underside of her jaw, the delicate well at the base of her throat, the slope of her shoulder, the bend of her elbow, the pulse beating heavily underneath the pale skin of her wrist, her palms and fingertips. He lavished time and care and infinite attention on all those soft delicate parts of a woman that aren't generally considered erogenous zones, but indisputably are.

She kissed him back the same way, trailing her lips over his eyelids and cheekbones, over his chiseled jaw and the strong curve of his neck where it melded into the swelling strength of his shoulder. She kissed the hair-dusted curve of his pectorals, his sinewy arms, his hard, callused, clever hands.

The fire took a long time to build and when it caught, finally, it was the slow-burning kind that pulsed with a deep incinerating heat, instead of the raging wildfire they were used to generating between them. Their movements were fluid and unhurried, there on the big cool bed in the anonymous motel room. They kissed and caressed and fondled with languorous deliberation, awash in sensation and sensuality. When he slipped into her, it was without haste, without the frantic urge to possess. He gave to her instead, his powerful thrusts deep and gentle and slow. There was no driving need to race to completion, for either of them, no desperately raging desire to have it happen *now, now, now!* The climax, when it came, was as gentle, as devastatingly tender, as deep and pulsating and lingering as what had gone before.

Her body arched up from the bed in a long sensuous curve as her orgasm rolled through her, rippling outward from her vagina and clitoris until every part of her body was tingling with sensation. She said his name, just once, longingly, lovingly, achingly, an inarticulate plea for even more closeness.

He put his hands beneath her back, supporting her, lifting her against him, pressing her tingling body to his chest, holding her close as his own body contracted in a deep, delicious orgasm of utter completion.

"Roxanne," he said, and kissed her.

Magic, indeed.

9

THERE WAS A FREE PANCAKE breakfast in downtown Cheyenne the next morning. It was, of course, packed. No cowboy worth his salt was going to turn down free made-from-scratch pancakes and freshly brewed coffee. Long picnic tables covered with cheerful blue-and-white-checked tablecloths had been set up in the plaza between the shops. Smiling cooks in cowboy hats and white aprons manned the large rectangular griddles—easily four feet by two feet—situated at each end of the dining area. The tantalizing smells of coffee, maple syrup and sizzling pork sausage filled the air. A rodeo clown offered free face painting for the dozens of kids running around. The place was packed.

Roxanne settled into a seat at one of the long picnic tables, saving their places while Tom stood in line. From there she saw a whole different side of the cowboys she'd gradually been coming to know over the past few weeks.

Tug Stiles, one of the wildest, rowdiest cowboys on the circuit, ate his breakfast with a pink-cheeked toddler sitting on his lap and an adoring young wife by his side. Clay Madison sat between his beaming parents, who had driven in from Nebraska to watch their

son compete. Even Rooster had a lady friend with
him, a sweet-faced waitress from Laramie who'd
taken the day off from work so she could spend it
with him.

"Most cowboys have wives and kids, just like
everyone else," Tom said, answering the question im-
plicit in her lifted eyebrow as he came back to the
table with their breakfast. He pried the lid off of one
of the cups of coffee he'd brought and handed it to
her—the requisite one-half teaspoon of sugar already
stirred into it—then inserted himself into the bench
seat beside her. "And those that aren't married have
sweethearts." He took an appreciative sip of his own
heavily sugared and creamed coffee. "Or parents,"
he said, with a friendly nod at Mr. and Mrs. Madison.
"Frontier Days gives them a chance to spend some
time together. Lots of rodeo families make this their
annual vacation every year for just that reason."

Sitting there, eating her breakfast of pancakes and
little link sausages, watching the cowboys she thought
she'd come to know so well interact with their families, she realized she didn't really know them at all.
Never in a million years would she have believed
those rough-and-ready, devil-may-care loners could
look so pathetically happy to have their families close
by. It very nearly brought tears to her eyes to see big
Tug Stiles bent so attentively over his tiny daughter,
feeding her bites of pancake off the end of his fork.
Or the way Clay Madison preened and purred under
loving attention of his proud parents. She hadn't realized until just this moment how desperately lonely
the cowboy life was, for both the cowboys and their

families—which made it all the more puzzling to her why anyone would choose to live this way.

What was it about the rodeo that made it so attractive to these men?

"Why do you do it?" she asked Tom again as they strolled hand-in-hand through the carnival midway on their way to the arena. "And don't give me that glory business. I'd like to hear the truth, please."

"That *is* the truth."

She gave him a skeptical look, lips pursed, eyebrows raised, the kind of look she gave her fifth graders back in Connecticut when she thought they were being less than completely forthcoming with their answers.

"Honest," he said, giving her the same earnest look her students did.

"Explain."

"I don't know if I can, exactly."

"You don't have to be exact," she said. "I'm just looking for a little insight, is all."

"Well…" He took a moment or two to gather his thoughts. "I guess what it all boils down to, really, is that for most cowboys the rodeo embodies the myth of the West, the way it used to be. Or—" he slanted a wry glance at her "—the way we *think* it used to be, which amounts to the same thing. Rodeo is John Wayne driving the cattle herd to the railhead in Abilene in *Red River*, or Gary Cooper walking down the middle of the street in *High Noon*, doing the hard thing because it's the right thing. For those eight seconds in the arena, a cowboy gets to live the legend. He gets to *be* the legend, a living, breathing icon of the American West. And not just in his own mind, either, but in the minds of the crowd, too, because we were all brought up on the myth. We all believe it to some extent. Even sophisticated east-coast city girls like you." He slanted another glance at her, wondering if he'd revealed too much of the man under the myth to a woman who saw him only as a summer fling. "Maybe, even, especially sophisticated east-coast city girls."

Roxanne knew exactly what he was getting at. She'd come West looking for a cowboy, looking for the myth, and found her own particular version of it in him. Six feet of lean, well-muscled male in a cowboy hat and tight-fitting jeans. He walked beside her now, the quintessence of every movie cowboy she'd ever seen or dreamed about. His bronc saddle was slung over one broad shoulder, his index finger hooked under the fork where the saddle horn would be if it had one. He'd buckled on his chaps and spurs before they left their motel room instead of carrying them, too. The chaps were made of battered, natural-colored leather, with a modest fringe and a widely spaced row of silver conchas down the outside of each leg. They flapped gently around his long, lean horseman's legs, framing the bulge beneath his fly and his tight cowboy butt. The little silver jingle-bobs on his spurs sang a sweet cowboy song with every step. Just looking at him made her breath catch and her heart beat faster.

Did that make her shallow? Or just susceptible?

"Who said I was from the east coast?" she asked, avoiding, for the moment, the question of her character. "I could be from Denver. Or Dallas." She laid the accent on extra thick and fluttered her eyelashes at him. "Or even San Antonio."

"Not with that accent, you couldn't," he said, deadpan. "Besides, you told me yourself you're from Connecticut."

Well, yes, there was that. "Did it ever fool you?" she said, getting back to the matter of the accent. She'd thought it had sounded pretty authentic—when she remembered to use it, that is. "Even for a minute?"

"Maybe for a minute." He slanted a glance down at her. "Did you want to fool me?"

She lifted one shoulder in a quasishrug. "Not really," she admitted, knowing in her heart of hearts that the only one she'd been trying to fool—was *still* trying to fool—was herself. "I thought it went with the look."

"The look?"

"You know, the yahoo-ride-'em-cowgirl look."

He stopped walking to look down at her. "Are you kidding? You think you look like a cowgirl?"

"Don't I?"

He shook his head. "Madison Avenue's idea of a cowgirl, maybe. In one of those sexy ads for designer jeans."

She looked down at herself. "These jeans are *not* designer," she said indignantly.

"No, they're Levi's," he said, humoring her. "Cowboys—and girls—wear Wrangler. And that hat looks like it just came out of the box. Plus, you're wearing it set back on your head like some greenhorn hayseed.'' He hefted the saddle from his shoulder with a twist of his wrist and bent at the knees, setting it gently on the ground between them, then reached out and grabbed her hat by the brim with both hands. Flexing the bendable wires in the straw brim, he reshaped it so that the sides flared up a bit and the front and back dipped down, and set it back on her head, making sure it tilted forward. ''That's the way you wear a cowboy hat.''

''Well, why didn't you tell me before?'' she said, wishing she had a mirror so she could see how it looked. ''Instead of letting me run around looking like a hayseed?''

''I thought that's the look you were aiming for.''

''Ha. Ha.'' She stuck her tongue out at him. ''Any other fashion faux pas you neglected to tell me about?''

''Well, now that you mention it…''

''What?''

''Those boots.'' He shook his head in mock consternation. ''Look around you, Slim. You see anybody else in bright-red cowboy boots?''

''But I got them at Neiman's in Dallas.''

''I rest my case,'' he said, and bent down to retrieve his saddle.

''Tug Stiles's boots are purple with yellow roses on the sides.''

''You gonna take fashion cues from a guy who has a lightning bolt sewn on the crotch of his jeans?''

He had a point. ''So, what color should I get? Brown? Black?'' She glanced around, checking out the footwear of the other people on the midway. ''Or should I just go step in a couple of cow patties and muddy these up a little?''

''You don't need new boots. And you don't need to step in any cow patties.''

''But you said—''

''I was just teasing you, Slim.'' He slung his saddle over his shoulder and reached for her hand, enfolding it in his once again. ''And you know how much I love to tease you,'' he said, giving her a smoldering look and that sexy cowboy grin of his that set her susceptible city girl's heart to beating erratically.

THAT NIGHT after the rodeo there was a free chili cook-off. A cowboy would no more pass up free chili than he would free pancakes, especially when there was a beer tent set up close by and a country-western band providing background music. Roxanne had washed and fluffed her hair, leaving her remodeled cowboy hat back in the motel room to avoid hat head, and changed into her short denim skirt and a sleeveless scoop-necked camisole in anticipation of the dancing that would come later, after dinner.

''You know what they say about why cowboys like chili so much, don't you?'' Tom said as they sat down at the wooden picnic tables—covered with red-and-white-checked oilcloth this time instead of the blue—with their favorite picks of the various chili offerings.

''No,'' she said, playing along. ''What do they say?''

''Chili's like sex. When is good, it's great. And when it's bad, it's still pretty good.''

Rooster snickered as if he'd never heard the joke

before. He'd been swapping stories and slapping backs at the beer tent and was in a jovial mood. "You know who makes good chili?" he said after he'd gotten over his glee. "That Jo Beth over at the Diamond J. That little gal makes a right good chili. Hot enough to sear through the roof of your mouth if you ain't careful. You said so yourself, remember?" He smiled happily at Tom, oblivious to the discouraging scowl on his partner's face. "At the barbecue her folks had last spring when she graduated from A&M? You said she made the best chili you ever tasted. Remember?"

"I remember," Tom said through his teeth.

Rooster might have been oblivious to Tom's displeasure, but Roxanne wasn't. "Who's Jo Beth?" she said, looking back and forth between the two men.

Tom shoveled a spoonful of chili into his mouth.

"Jo Beth Jensen," Rooster supplied, happy to be of service. "Her daddy's spread runs right alongside of the Second Chance. Nice little gal. Sweet as cherry pie and as pretty as a newborn foal. Smart, too. Got herself a degree in— What was it she got her schoolin' in, Tom?"

"Animal science," he muttered, wishing Rooster would shut the hell up about Jo Beth. "How's your chili?"

"Chili's fine," Rooster said, and turned back to Roxanne. "She aims to take over the Diamond J someday. Well, she'll have to, won't she, seein' as how she's her mama and daddy's only chick. Someday, some lucky man's goin' get himself a nice little wife *and* the Diamond J." He waggled his eyebrows suggestively, grinning at Tom through a beery haze. "Ain't that right, pard?"

"I wouldn't know." Tom pushed his bowl away and rose from the table. "Come on, Slim." He grabbed Roxanne's hand, pulling her to her feet. "Let's dance."

THEY CIRCLED the makeshift dance floor a couple of times in silence, their booted feet scuffing along the bare wooden planks, his right hand curved around her neck under her tousled blond hair, her left thumb hooked in the belt loop on the side of his jeans. Their clasped hands were held low at their sides, in classic country style, as he guided her backward around the crowded floor. It was the perfect setting for romance. The air was soft and warm. The twilight sky was just beginning to fill with stars. The band was doing a credible rendition of George Strait's heartfelt cowboy lament "Does Fort Worth Ever Cross Your Mind?" as they moved together over the floor.

Tom danced with his jaw clenched and his gaze fixed firmly on a point somewhere over her right shoulder, wishing he'd never heard the name Jo Beth Jensen, wishing to hell Slim had never heard it, either. Roxanne stared at the faint white scar on his chin and wondered if she should just keep her mouth shut.

What did it matter who Jo Beth Jensen was? And what difference did it make if she was smart and pretty and could make a "right good" bowl of chili? And so what if her daddy's "spread" ran alongside Tom's?

It wasn't as if she—Roxanne—had any real claim

on him, or even wanted one, if it came to that. Their affair had very definite limits. To the end of the summer and that was it. That's what they'd agreed to. No fuss. No muss. No strings. Once the summer was over she'd pack up and go back to Connecticut where she belonged, putting her Wild West adventure behind her. And he could go back to his "spread" in wherever Texas and marry his neighbor's horse-faced daughter and raise a whole passel of horse-faced kids, and...

"Are you the lucky man who's going to marry Jo Beth and get himself a nice little wife *and* the Diamond J?" she said snidely, unable to keep her mouth shut, after all. A month of speaking her mind freely had obviously left its mark.

His gaze flickered to hers. "I'm not engaged to her, if that's what you're asking," he said defensively, and looked away again.

"I wouldn't care if you were," she lied. "I was just wondering, is all."

That got his undivided attention. "You wouldn't care if I was engaged?" His expression was indignant and disbelieving. "Are you saying you'd knowingly sleep with a man who was engaged to another woman?"

She wanted to lie again, wanted to shrug it off with a laugh and an insouciant toss of her head, but she couldn't. "Yes, of course, I'd care! I *do* care. And, no, I wouldn't knowingly sleep with a man who was engaged to another woman. In fact, I'd be inclined to *geld* a man who put me in that position." She smiled with saccharine sweetness. "And I'd use the dullest knife I could find to do it."

"You can put your knife away, Slim. I'm not engaged to her."

"Are you going steady?"

"No, we're not going steady. Cowboys don't go steady. We keep company."

"So, are you keeping company with her?"

"No, I'm not keeping company with her. We've never even dated."

"Well, then…" She looked up at him, a puzzled expression in her whiskey-colored eyes. "I don't understand. If you're not involved with her why the guilt trip when Rooster mentioned her name?"

Tom gave it his best shot. "It's against the cowboy code to talk about one woman when he's with another, is all. Bad manners. If Rooster hadn't had a few brews too many he would have been more gentlemanly and not mentioned her."

Roxanne didn't believe that for a minute. She'd been around cowboys long enough to know they'd talk about any woman, any time, anywhere. Just like any other man. "What a load of B.S.," she scoffed.

"That's my story and I'm sticking to it," Tom said, and twirled her in series of quick spin turns in the hopes she'd get dizzy and forget what they'd been talking about.

But Roxanne was made of sterner stuff. "You've thought about it, though, haven't you?" she said, resuming their conversation right where she'd left off when he brought her back in against his chest again.

"That's why you reacted like a kid who'd got caught with his hand in the cookie jar."

"Thought about what?"

"Marrying little miss Texas A&M with the degree in animal science and her daddy's spread as a dowry."

"I wouldn't marry a woman for money," he said, insulted.

"What would you marry her for, then?"

"A life partner," he said instantly, like a man who'd recently given it a lot of thought and didn't have to pick and choose his words now. "Someone who could understand and share my life. Someone to raise a family with. Build a future with. Grow old with."

Someone like you, he thought, surprising himself.

He stumbled and missed a step, causing them to bump shoulders with another pair of dancers. "Beg pardon," he mumbled, wondering where the hell *that* had come from.

She wasn't the kind of woman he had in mind to marry. Not by a long shot. The kind of woman he had in mind to marry was, well…he suddenly wasn't sure exactly what kind of woman he had in mind. He'd thought it had been someone like Jo Beth but, suddenly, someone like Jo Beth seemed kind of tame and uninteresting and dull. Still, a prudent man didn't marry a woman like Slim. She was a good-time girl, a buckle bunny who picked up cowboys in bars and took them back to her motel room for wild raucous sex. Except that she wasn't…quite. He was the only cowboy she'd picked up, after all, and she hadn't so much as smiled at another cowboy with anything like invitation in her eyes, despite that little misunderstanding they'd had about Clay Madison. No, the way she treated the other cowboys—Clay, included—was almost, well, motherly. And she'd become like a big sister to Rooster, chiding him about his diet, fretting over his injuries, reading him bedtime stories, for God's sake!

Were those the actions of a die-hard buckle bunny?

But, then, hell, he thought, even if they weren't, what difference did it make, anyway? So what if there was more to her than he'd thought that first night in Lubbock? So what if she was more than sass and sex and sweetness? Forever wasn't part of their deal. He was just a summer fling, a part of her Wild West adventure, and in six weeks she'd be leaving him to go back to her real life. The thought gave him an odd, uneasy feeling in the center of his chest. He didn't think he'd be ready to let her go in six weeks. Not in six months. Hell, maybe not ever...

"And Jo Beth is that someone?" she prodded, unable to let it go.

He gave her a blank look. "Someone who what?" he said, still trying to sort it all out in his mind. He had to let her go, of course. He *would* let her go. That was their deal, and it had been his plan from the get-go. Neither of them was looking for anything permanent...

"Someone you might marry," she said, exasperated.

"Well...ah..." With an effort, he shook off his distraction. "I guess I've sort of considered that she could be,'' he admitted, wondering how he'd ever thought that possible. He certainly wasn't considering it now.

''Aha!'' Roxanne pounced on that like a barn cat on a mouse. ''I *knew* it! You *have* thought about marrying her!''

''I haven't thought about marrying her, specifically,'' he said, backtracking for all he was worth. ''I've just been thinking about getting married in a general kind of way. And what with her living right next door, so to speak, Jo Beth was just one of the possibilities.''

''Oh, really?'' Her eyebrows disappeared into her bangs. Her chin came up in that way that tempted and challenged him. ''And just how many other possibilities are there?''

Tom tightened his grip on her right hand and moved in closer, in case she took it into her head to try to sucker punch him again. ''For crying out loud, Slim. Do you mean to take everything I say the wrong way?''

''You said Jo Beth was only *one* of the possibilities. How else am I supposed to take it except to mean there are others?'' She narrowed her eyes at him. ''I don't like being one of a crowd.''

''You're not one of a crowd, damn it. You're one of a kind. For which I am profoundly grateful. I don't think the world could handle more than one of you.'' He was on the hairy edge of exasperation, his tone colored with unwilling amusement, hovering somewhere between frustrated and admiring. ''I know I sure as hell couldn't.''

Roxanne ignored the exasperation and focused on the admiration. ''You think I'm one of a kind?'' She leaned into him, all the fight gone out of her, and smiled up into his face. ''Really?''

''Really,'' he said, and gathered her in close, dropping her hand to wrap both arms around her.

She sighed and snuggled into him like a kitten in familiar hands, her own arms lifting to circle his waist, her head on his shoulder, her face nestled into the warm curve of his neck.

They danced without speaking for several long minutes, feet shuffling over the wooden dance floor, bodies swaying under the stars, hearts beating in time to the music and the slow, sweet pulse of unhurried passion, content for the moment merely to hold each other and be. And then he lifted his head, and she lifted hers, and they stared at each other, intently, like lovers staring at each other across the width of a pillow.

''I want you,'' he said, and wondered if he meant for now, or forever. ''So much.''

''I know.'' She touched her lips to his. ''I want you, too.''

He smiled.

And she smiled.

And without another word they turned and, hand-in-hand, left the dance floor.

They continued to hold hands in the cab of the truck on the way back to the motel. They held hands on the short walk from the truck to their room. They were still holding hands—both hands now when they stood face-to-face beside the bed, palm to palm, fingers intertwined—when he leaned down and kissed her.

It was a soft, sweet kiss, his lips barely brushing across hers…lifting away…coming back for a second taste…a third…the pressure increasing slightly then, but still gently, almost hesitantly, as if it were the first kiss between them, as if he had just discovered the promise of passion in her and was testing its depths. Entranced, Roxanne answered in kind, her kisses as soft, as gentle, as giving as his, until, finally, gentleness wasn't enough and she opened her mouth to him, inviting a deeper possession, a closer communion, a more complete union.

He wrapped his arms around her, bringing her body flush against his, taking their clasped hands to the small of her back, and slanted his mouth across hers, deepening the kiss. He used his tongue now, but still softly, still sweetly, the subtle seducer rather than the bold invader. Roxanne sighed and let herself be seduced.

His kisses trailed from her lips to her jaw to the soft sensitive place behind her ear, slowly—oh, so slowly—sliding down the long, slender column of her neck to the valley between her breasts. As he had once before, he buried his nose there and simply breathed her in, as if the very smell of her intoxicated him.

And, as she had before, Roxanne shuddered in his arms and fell a little bit in love. Not all the way in love, she cautioned herself. Not all the way, but just a little bit. Just enough to make her breath catch and her heart beat faster. Just enough to make her dizzy with need.

"Tom." It was the only word she could think of to say. The only word that made any sense at the moment. "Tom."

He raised his head and stared down into her flushed face. Her lips were slicked and red from his kisses. Her eyes were nearly golden in the dim light, her pupils large and round and focused intently on his face. "You're so damned beautiful," he murmured. "And I want you so damned much."

"Then take me." Her head fell back in surrender. "I'm yours. Take me."

His eyes flared wide, passion and heat and something else warring in their hot blue depths. He let go of her hands and stooped, lifting her into his arms so he could lower her to the bed. She expected him to fall upon her, then, to shove the necessary bits and pieces of clothing out of the way and ride her, wildly, as he had so many times before. Instead, he straightened and began undressing himself. He dropped his clothes where he stood; his hat, his boots, his shirt and jeans and underclothes were all discarded, falling like leaves onto the carpeted floor, as she lay there and watched, mesmerized. When he was naked, he began undressing her.

He removed her boots first, dropping them on the floor at the foot of the bed. He unzipped her little denim skirt and tugged it off her hips and down the length of her bare legs. And then he sat down on the edge of the bed, bypassing her panties, and reached for the first button on her white eyelet camisole.

His gaze locked with hers, something more than passion still burning in his eyes as he slowly unbut-

toned her blouse and spread it open. Her underwear
was new, purchased on her whirlwind shopping trip
to Wal-Mart the week before. The fabric was old-
fashioned and sweet, white cotton lace with tiny blue
forget-me-nots embroidered on it. The cut was scan-
dalous—brief and unabashedly sexy. The whole was
as much a dichotomy as the woman who wore it.

"So beautiful," he said, and bent down, pressing
his lips to the plump swell of flesh above the edge of
the bra. "I want you."

There was an edge of desperation in his voice, a
need she had never heard before, a something that set
her blood to racing through her veins, and her mind
to weaving impossible fantasies. She lifted her hands
up to his head, threading her fingers through his thick
dark hair. "I want you, too," she whispered, and
brought his mouth down to hers for a searing, open-
mouthed kiss.

The loving that followed was hot and intense, incredibly wild, impossibly tender. And when he was
finally positioned between her silky thighs, on the
verge of taking what they both wanted so desperately,
their hands were linked, palm to palm, fingers entwined, pressed into the mattress on either side of her
head.

"I want you," he said as he thrust into her.

A HOT, SWEATY, tempestuous hour later, they lay,
skin to skin, heart to heart, in the middle of the rumpled motel bed.

"I'm sorry about the third degree tonight," Roxanne murmured into the damp curve of his neck.

"I'm not." Tom ran his hand down the length of her bare back to the curve of her equally bare bottom, and gave it a little squeeze. "Every time you throw one of your little hissy fits, we have really hot make-up sex."

Too relaxed to manage a more forceful display of feminine ire for his chauvinistic remark, she bit him lightly on the neck. "No, really, I mean it. I'm sorry." She kissed the place she'd bitten and raised up, crossing her arms over his chest so she could look down into his face. "I have no right to pry into your personal life. What you did before this summer and what you do after it isn't any of my business," she said, as much to remind herself of that fact as to reassure him. "You're only required to be a one-woman man while we're together."

"I reckon I'm pretty much a one-woman man all the time, anyway," he said, wondering if, from now on, that one woman was going to be her. Wondering, too, what the hell he was going to do about it if that were the case. "One at a time is about all I can handle." He grinned at her. "Especially when that one is a tall cool glass of water with a hair-trigger temper and a mean right jab."

"I do not have a hair-trigger temper."

He raised an eyebrow.

"It's your own fault, anyway," she said, and tweaked his chest hairs.

"How do you figure that?"

"You're the only person I've ever hit in my entire life, so it must be your fault."

"Isn't that called blaming the victim?"

"Victim, my ass."

"And it's such a nice ass, too," he said, and pinched it.

She squealed and tweaked his chest hairs again, harder this time so that he yelped in response. "See? You *made* me do that. I'm not normally a violent per—" The last word was muffled against his chest as he surged upward and rolled her beneath him.

A brief but vigorous tussle ensued. They wrestled across the bed like rambunctious children, Roxanne squirming and squealing, Tom trying mostly to keep her from pinching anything vital. In his effort to evade her grasping fingers, he rolled too near the edge of the bed and toppled off onto the floor, dragging Roxanne down with him. She snagged a pillow as she went over and was up on her knees in an instant, pummeling him with it before he had to a chance to catch his breath.

"Dang, woman." He cupped his hands over his privates. "Watch your knee."

"Say uncle." She bashed him in the head with the pillow. "Say it."

"Uncle."

She checked her next blow, surprised by his easy capitulation. That quick, he snatched the pillow out of her hands, tossed it aside, and reversed their positions. Flat on her back on the floor, her arms held down on either side of her head, her chest heaving with exertion, Roxanne went limp. "What now, sugar?" she said, and batted her eyelashes at him.

"Now, we have *really* hot make-up sex," he said, and lowered his mouth to hers.

She bit his lip.

"And you say you're not a violent person," he chided, lust and laughter sparkling in his blue eyes as he stared down at her.

Roxanne stared back, breathless with laughter, flushed with arousal, waiting for what he would do next.

He got a cagey, considering look in his eyes. "You know what happens to violent little girls, don't you?"

"No," she said, her eyes glittering with anticipation. "What happens to them?"

"They get punished." He grinned evilly. "Severely."

There was a long beat of silence as they stared at each other. The air between them was ripe with expectation and excitement, the thrill of the forbidden, the lure of the illicit. It was like that first moment between them at Ed Earl's all over again, that moment when they stared into each other's eyes from a distance of inches, with the sexual energy crackling back and forth like heat lightning, and wondered if they were going to end up spending the night together. And now, as she had then, Roxanne provided exactly the prod he needed to make his move.

"You wouldn't dare," she said, all the while hoping desperately that he would.

Tom not only dared, he did.

Without letting go of her wrists, he heaved himself to his feet, sat down on the edge of the bed and jerked her, facedown, across his lap. She squirmed in excitement and delicious libidinous fear. His hand came down on her bare bottom with a sharp smacking sound. It stung a bit more than she expected it to.

She reared up in surprise. "Hey, that hurt!"

"That was for sucker punching me at the rodeo in Santa Fe," he said, pushing her back down with a hand on the top of her head. He smacked her again, not quite so hard, but still with enough force to make her skin tingle and redden. "And that was for dancing with that clown in the Bare Back Saloon and letting him hold you too damn close. And that—" he smacked her a third time "—was for kissing Clay right under my nose."

"Stop!" She squirmed against his thighs, but made no real effort to get away. She could feel his erection against her stomach, as rock-hard and ready as if they hadn't just made love. Her own body was practically dripping with desire. "Stop it right now."

"Are you going to be good?" He brought his hand down again, lightly this time, caressingly, shaping his palm over the satin skin of her bottom. It was as rosy as the valentine it resembled, as hot as the sun-baked sand of the desert.

"Yes." Instinctively, without conscious thought or design, she arched her back, thrusting her tingling posterior up against the curve of his hand, exposing the glistening pink folds of her sex. "Yes, I'll be good."

"You sure you know how?"

"Yes. Yes, I know how. I'll be good," she said, nearly panting with excitement. "I promise."

He slipped his hand down between her legs. "How good?" he asked, and slid a finger into her.

She nearly came right then and there. Her breath caught in her throat as she tried, and failed, to stifle a whimper.

"How good?" he asked again.

"How good do you want me to be?"

"Only as good as you want to be." He withdrew his hand from between her legs and let her slide to her knees beside him. "How good do you want to be, Slim?"

She put her hands on his thighs and looked up at him from under her lashes. "Good enough to make you beg for mercy."

Tom leaned back on his elbows. "I dare you," he said.

Her gaze locked with his, Roxanne smiled and slowly, inch by excruciating inch, slid her hands up his hair-dusted thighs to his groin. Despite his deliberately relaxed position, she could feel the coiled tension in his long, lanky body, see it in the clenched muscles of his hard thighs and abdomen. His penis was nearly parallel to his stomach, pointing straight up at his navel. It jerked when she touched it.

"Aw, isn't that cute," she said to cover her own nervousness. "He's shy." She curled her hand around his shaft and, very gently, brought it upright. "I'll be gentle," she promised, and bent her head.

She'd never done this but a few times before, and not very successfully, judging by the reaction of her partner at the time. She suspected it was mostly because she hadn't really wanted to do it. Now, she did. And now, she wanted to be very, very good at it. She wanted to make him beg, as he had made her beg.

She began by kissing the round plum-shaped head, tentatively at first and then, as he indicated his pleasure, with more confidence. She progressed to little catlike licks, moved on to long, leisurely swipes with the flat of her tongue until, finally—when he was on his back and clutching the bedspread in his fists—she had pity on him and took him into her mouth.

"Please," he said, when she had tortured him for several minutes. Sweat beaded his upper lip and dampened the dark, crinkly hair on his chest. "Please."

She raised her head. "Please what?"

He reached down and grasped her by the shoulders, pulling her up the length of his body. "Ride me," he said, holding his shaft so she could mount.

She swung her leg over his supine body, straddling him, and impaled herself.

They both closed their eyes against the exquisite pleasure of it, savoring the feeling of unity and oneness. And then she leaned forward, putting her hands on his slick, sweaty chest for balance, and began to move against him, raising and lowering her hips as if she were riding a horse at a rising trot.

She'd only ever done this a few times before, too, because the other half of her former mature adult relationship hadn't favored the woman-on-top position. She found that she liked it very much, indeed. It gave her a freedom she'd never had before, allowing her to control the depth and the speed and the angle of penetration. She experimented, swiveling her hips first one way, then the other...slowing down and speeding up…varying the rhythm until she found the one that made Tom suck in his breath and whimper.

"Sweet Lord in heaven!" He hissed the words out between clenched teeth as his body rose and tightened, exploding in a rapturous climax.

Roxanne had just started to follow him over into bliss when the phone rang.

It wasn't the hotel phone on the bedside table. It was his cell phone, the one he kept clipped to the belt on his jeans, except when he rode. Roxanne had seen him use it to call ahead to the rodeo to find out what horse he'd drawn, or to make a motel reservation when they rolled into town late at night, but she'd never heard it ring before.

"I'm sorry," he said, as he tipped her sideways onto the bed. "I have to answer that."

10

___

"How bad is it?" Tom was sitting on the edge of the bed, the phone tucked awkwardly between his ear and shoulder as he dragged on his underwear and jeans. "What does the doctor say? Surgery? When? Why so soon? No, that's all right, Augie. Don't worry about it. I'll talk to the doctor myself as soon as I get there. You and the other kids go on back to the ranch and keep on with your regular routine." He pulled on his socks and boots, and stood to fasten his jeans. "Yes, I know, but try. The Padre would want it that way. You know he would." He grabbed his shirt from the floor and shrugged into it, one arm at a time, as he listened to the slightly hysterical voice on the other end of the line. "It's going to be all right, Augie. You and the boys just sit tight and try not to worry. I'll be there as soon as I can and we'll all get through this together. Tell the Padre to hang in there." He flipped the phone closed. "We've got a family emergency," he said to Roxanne as he headed for the door. "I've got to go roust Rooster out of bed and let him know what's going on."

Roxanne jumped up from the middle of the bed where she had been kneeling, watching him through-out the telephone conversation. Grabbing one of the blankets off of the floor to wrap around her naked body, she followed him to the door, wondering what was going on. Augie? The Padre? The other kids? Were they his brothers? His children? The fact that she didn't know brought home to her how little she really knew about him.

"Come on, Rooster." Tom pounded on the door of the adjoining room. "Haul your ass out of bed. We've got trouble."

There was a thumping noise, then a muffled curse, and Rooster appeared at the door. He was blinking and bleary-eyed, his short brown hair sticking up in all directions. He was holding on to his head with both hands. "What's all the racket about?" he demanded querulously. "Where's the fire?"

"I just got a call from home. The Padre's had a heart attack."

"A heart attack?" Rooster scrubbed at his face with both hands as if that would help him absorb the news. "The Padre had a heart attack? When?"

"A couple of hours ago. Augie called me from the hospital."

"How bad?"

"Bad enough, from what Augie said. They almost lost him a couple of times before they got him stabilized, but he's resting comfortably now—whatever the hell that means—and they've got him scheduled for a triple by-pass first thing in the morning."

"Sweet baby Jesus!" Rooster swore softly.

"I'm going to call around, see if I can find some kind of charter flight that will get me home before the surgery. Otherwise I'll take a commercial flight into Dallas and drive from there.''

Rooster nodded. "It'll only take me a minute to get my gear together.''

"There's no need for you to go, too. No, hear me out," Tom said, as Rooster started to protest. "It only needs one of us to ride herd on the kids and see that everything's running smooth. You've got to be here for the finals on Sunday, and then Wichita the day after that, and Oklahoma City the day after that.''

"But—''

"The Padre'll understand. And he isn't going to care much, anyway, about who is or isn't pacing around in the waiting room.''

"Maybe you should be the one to stay for the finals," Rooster said, when he could get a word in edgewise. "You've been scorin' good all week. An', hell, I got this bum knee slowin' me down, anyway.''

"Not so's anyone would notice," Tom said dryly, seeing through the ploy. Rooster's knee hadn't given him a lick of trouble since they got to Cheyenne; he'd pulled down some of the best scores of his life that week.

"Besides, I got a good five, ten years of rodeoing in me yet," Rooster said. "I don't make it to Vegas this year, there's always next. But this is your last chance an' it's a damned good one. You pull down a winning score in the finals on Sunday and you're in the top fifteen, guaranteed. I should be the one to turn out," he said earnestly. "I know how much it means to you to get to Vegas before you retire.''

"Not as much as it means to you," Tom said. "I

never wanted it as much as you. Ever. That's why I've been content to be a circuit cowboy all my life. Here—'' he handed Rooster the cell phone. ''You keep this with you and I'll call you the minute he comes out of surgery.'' He dug into the pocket of his jeans. ''And here's the keys to the truck. I'll expect to see it, and you, in Bowie next week after you kick butt in Oklahoma City. The Padre ought to be back home by then—'' he smiled crookedly ''—and we'll all be about ready to have a new face around to keep him from driving everybody crazy.''

Considering the subject closed, he turned away without waiting for an answer, and headed back to his room. Roxanne stepped back, out of the way, as he brushed past her, then stood awkwardly, unsure of what to do, watching as he dug the Yellow Pages out of the drawer of the bedside dresser and set about arranging a charter flight to Bowie, Texas.

This was the end, then, she thought forlornly, trying desperately not to cry. He was going to fly home to deal with a family emergency and she was going to— What? Go back to Connecticut? She didn't *want* to go back to Connecticut. Her vacation wasn't over, damn it! She still had a few fantasies she hadn't fulfilled. And she wasn't nearly ready to say goodbye to her good-looking dangerous cowboy.

Not yet.

Maybe not ever, she thought, and realized that the San Antonio barrel racer had been dead on the money; she probably *was* going to get her poor little heart broken—and a lot sooner than she'd anticipated, too.

"You'd better get moving," he said as he hung up the phone. "The plane leaves in less than an hour."

"You want me to come with you?" she said, hardly daring to hope.

"Well, I thought…" But the thing was, he realized as she stood there, staring at him with an incredulous look on her face, he *hadn't* thought. He'd assumed. He wanted her to go with him, ergo she must want it, too. Simple as that. Except why the hell would a woman like her want to fly down to Bowie, Texas, while he nurse-maided a sick old man and rode herd on a bunch of rowdy kids?

On the other hand, he wouldn't be playing nurse-maid the entire time and the kids were a self-sufficient bunch, and what was between the two of them was still as hot—hotter—that it had been that first night in Lubbock. Why *wouldn't* she want to go with him?

"I thought we had an agreement," he said, finally, because he didn't know what else to say. "We've got nearly six weeks to go on it."

"You want me to come with you?" she said again.

"Well, it wouldn't set right on my conscience to leave you by yourself in Cheyenne. And I'm pretty sure you don't want to finish out the season riding shotgun with Rooster. Do you?"

She shook her head.

"And if it turns out you don't like it in Bowie—" he shrugged to show it made no never mind to him "—Dallas is less than a hundred miles away. You can catch a plane to anywhere from there."

"I wouldn't by in the way?"

"Probably," he admitted. "But I want you there, anyway. I haven't near got my fill of you, yet."

And, God help him, he was beginning to think he never would.

THE PLANE that was going to take them to Bowie was a small twin-engine Cessna. They waited on uncomfortable orange plastic seats in a small, glassed-in lounge, watching through the window as the pilot conducted a thorough preflight inspection of the plane under the bright industrial lights shining down from the roof of the metal hangar.

"What did Rooster mean about you wanting to get to Vegas before you retire?" Roxanne said, trying to distract herself from the coming flight. She wasn't an enthusiastic air traveler at the best of times and the sight of the tiny Cessna had her nerves jumping.

Tom smiled distractedly, his gaze on the pilot and the plane, and squeezed her hand. "Vegas is where they hold the rodeo finals," he reminded her.

"I know that. I meant what did he mean about you retiring?"

"This is my last go-round. I'm officially hanging up my saddle at the end of the season."

"Why?"

He looked at her then. "Why does anybody retire? Because it's time."

"But you're only—what—thirty. Isn't that a little young to retire?"

He grinned. "Darlin', That's old for a cowboy. Damned old. And cowboyin' has never been my whole life, anyway. Not like it's been for Rooster.

Rodeo's always been more a hobby for me. I've mostly done it weekends, close to home, so's I could fit it in around my regular life as much as possible. Only full-time professional cowboys can rack up enough points to make Vegas."

"And that's what you wanted to do before you retired? Make the finals in Vegas?

He shrugged. "I thought it'd be fun to give it a shot. Make my last year something to remember. Really go hog wild." His grin flashed again, a little self-deprecating around the edges this time. "Have myself one last fling before I settle down."

"Settle down to what, exactly?"

"Marriage. Kids. All the normal, everyday things a man wants at the end of the day. We've got big plans to enlarge the school at the Second Chance so we can take in more kids. And I've got an experimental breeding program going on with Dan Jensen over at the Diamond J that I want to devote more time to. Can't do all that if I'm running off to the rodeo every weekend. So—" he shrugged "—I decided to give it one last shot. Just me and Rooster, going down the road together, living the footloose and fancy-free life of the professional rodeo cowboy before I packed it in and become entirely respectable."

"We're just about ready to take off, so if either of you folks need to visit the facilities before we head out, now's the time to do it," the pilot said, poking his head into the room before Roxanne could ask if she was part of that footloose and fancy-free life, that final fling.

She didn't really have to ask to know, though. Of

course, she was part of it. Wild sexual encounters were always a part of what final flings were all about. She knew that firsthand; wild sexual encounters with a good-looking dangerous cowboy had been an integral part of her own plans for a last fling.

So why did she feel so sad that their plans were so in sync? It was exactly what she wanted. Wasn't it?

"Slim?" Tom nudged her out of her abstraction. "You need to visit the ladies'? It's going to be a long flight and there's no facilities in the Cessna."

Although she didn't really feel the need to go, Roxanne headed for the "ladies'" on the theory that you should never pass up the opportunity to use the facilities. It was a little tidbit of wisdom she'd picked up living on the road; you never knew how far away the next bathroom would be, so it was better to grab every opportunity.

The pilot was already in his seat when she exited the hangar. Tom was standing next to the wing, waiting to hand her in. The plane only had four seats. Roxanne squeezed into the one behind the pilot. Tom put his saddle in the one beside the pilot and climbed into the back next to Roxanne. It was a tight fit, strapped in, noisy and uncomfortable. Because they had to wear headphones to communicate, any private conversation was impossible. All of the questions Roxanne was burning to ask Tom—about the life of respectability he envisioned for himself, about the Padre and the kids, about Jo Beth Jensen and how she fit into his plans—would have to wait until they were on the ground again.

"How long to Bowie?" Tom said, after the plane

was safely in the air and the pilot was free to make conversation.

"Eight hours, give or take, depending on the head-winds." The pilot's words crackled through the head-phones. "We should set down around seven, seven-thirty at the latest."

Tom nodded, then reached over, tapping Roxanne on the shoulder. He motioned for her to take off the headphones. "You should try to get some sleep," he said, his lips against her ear. "It's going to be chaos when we get there." He wrapped his arm around her shoulders, silently urging her to lean against him, and stared out the window at the darkness, never once closing his eyes during the entire trip.

THEY LANDED AT A SMALL private airstrip about ten miles outside of Bowie. Owned by a group of local ranchers, it consisted of two parallel runways and a single barnlike hangar planted smack-dab in the mid-dle of an empty field. There was a light on inside the hangar, despite the warm golden-pink glow of the ris-ing sun, and two pickups parked outside of it. One was a battered blue Dodge with the Second Chance brand painted on the side. The driver was waiting for them when the plane taxied up to the hangar. He rushed to the aircraft as soon as the propellers had stopped spinning and jerked the door open.

"Boy, am I glad to see you," he said, automatically reaching for the saddle Tom handed out to him. "The Padre's operation is at nine and I was afraid you weren't gonna get here on time. Miz Jenzen is out at the ranch with the kids. The Padre told me to call her to come over. He was talkin' pretty good last night after they got him settled in. He—''

''Hey, whoa, there now, Augie. Slow down, boy.'' Tom put his hand on the boy's shoulder and gave it a comforting squeeze. ''Take a deep breath before you hyperventilate.''

Augie smiled sheepishly and sucked in a breath, letting it whoosh out in a gusty sigh. ''I sure am glad to see you,'' he said again. His gaze darted to Roxanne as she stepped out onto the wing of the plane.

Tom turned around to hold out a hand to her and steady her descent. ''I'd like you to meet a friend of mine,'' he said to the boy when she was on the ground beside him. ''This is Miz Roxy Archer. Roxy, say hi to Augustine Chavez.''

The boy was tall, thin and gangly, more youthful-looking than the sixteen she knew he must be to be driving the pickup truck, with dark curly hair and liquid brown eyes that showed signs of sleeplessness and worry. He had a crudely fashioned tattoo peaking out from under the cuff of his shirt.

''Hello, Augie,'' she said politely, wondering what the relationship was between him and Tom. Not father and son, certainly, judging by the different last names. And probably not brothers, either, as there wasn't the slightest physical resemblance between them. ''It's a pleasure to meet you.''

''Ma'am,'' the boy said, the expression in his eyes wary and assessing.

Roxanne knew what he would see when he looked at her. She was rumpled and travel weary, her hair sticking all up anyhow from sleeping on Tom's shoul-

der, her lipstick chewed off, her face pale with the
faint nausea that came from flying in a small plane.
She had Tom's denim jacket slung over her shoulders,
hanging down over her snug red tank and city-slicker
jeans.

The boy dismissed her with a single disdainful
glance and turned his attention back to Tom. "I've
got a thermos of coffee and a sack of sausage biscuits
in the truck in case you're hungry," he said. "The
biscuits are from MacDonald's but Miz Jensen made
the coffee." His eyes flickered back to Roxanne for
an instant. "Only got one cup, though, from the top
of the thermos."

"One cup will do us just fine." Tom said. "Why
don't you go on and stow my saddle in the back of
the truck. We'll get the rest of the gear out of the hold
and be right behind you."

"I don't think he likes me," Roxanne whispered
as the boy headed toward the truck with the saddle
slung over his shoulder.

"He's just leery around people he doesn't know,"
Tom said. "Give him a few days, and he'll be talking
your ear off."

He certainly talked Tom's ear off, filling him on
the situation as they drove to the hospital. "He was
out in the corral with that little sorrel mare, Magpie.
You know the one with the freckled nose? She'd
snagged her left hock on a nail and he was out there
doctorin' her up when he suddenly just keeled over,
right there in the corral. He just up and keeled over,"
Augie said. "Scared the bejesus out of the new kid,
Jared. He came runnin' into the barn, all kinda white

in the eyes like a horse on loco weed, and said the Padre was havin' some kind of fit, and somebody better call 9-1-1. The ambulance got there right quick and the paramedics used those electric shock things on him. It'd been kinda cool to see if it hadn't been the Padre they were doing it to.''

By the time they pulled into the parking lot of the Bowie Community Hospital, Roxanne knew all about the Padre's condition, but nothing about who the Padre was or, more importantly, who he was to Tom.

TOM SAT WITH HIS FOREARMS balanced on his widespread knees, a cup of vending-machine coffee dangling between his hands. He'd just spent twenty grueling minutes with the surgeon, getting the lowdown on the upcoming by-pass operation, and another heart-wrenching ten holding the unresponsive hand of the elderly man who would be undergoing it. He was bone-tired and scared shitless.

Not knowing what else to do, how much he would let her do, Roxanne reached over and rubbed his back lightly. ''Talk to me,'' she said softly, her voice low in deference to Augie, who sat slumped sideways in his chair on the other side of Tom, sleeping off the long night of worry while they waited for the Padre to come out of surgery. ''Let me help.''

''His name is Hector Menendez,'' Tom said as if she'd asked. ''Everybody calls him Padre, though, because he studied for the priesthood when he was younger.'' He picked at the rim of the coffee cup with his thumb. ''He runs the Second Chance Ranch.''

"I thought the Second Chance was your place."

"No. The Second Chance belongs to the Padre. It's where I grew up. Or mostly, anyway." His gaze flickered up to her face and away. "It's a home for delinquent and abandoned boys."

Roxanne's eyes widened. "You were an abandoned child?"

"I was a delinquent child," he corrected. "My mother was barely fifteen when I was born. Unwed. Mostly uneducated. She did her best by me, but—" he shrugged "—her best wasn't very good back then. By the time I was ten, I was already getting into trouble with the police."

"What kind of trouble can a ten-year-old get into with the police?" Roxanne asked, her tone skeptical and disbelieving.

Which proved, he thought, how little experience she'd had with the seamier side of life. "Shoplifting. Vandalism. Truancy. All petty stuff, but the way I was going, I would have been a hardened felon by the time I was twelve if she hadn't turned me over to the Padre."

"She abandoned you?'

"She saved me," he said. "I was too much for her to handle and she knew it. The Padre gave me the kind of structured environment I needed. He gave me chores, taught me self-discipline and self-control, made sure I did my homework and went to school. If it weren't for him, I'd've ended up riding broncs at the Huntsville prison rodeo. Instead, I went on to college, became a teacher, made a decent life for myself."

"And your mother? What happened to her?"

"She moved to Dallas and got a job. Went to night school and got a better job. She's a nurse at Presbyterian Hospital now," he said, pride evident under the weariness in his tone. "Works in ER."

"Did you ever live with her again?"

Tom shook his head. "By the time she got herself together and could've made a home for the both of us, I was already in college."

"And your father? Where is he?"

"The Padre is all the father I've ever had. All the father I've ever needed," he said, and found himself suddenly fighting tears. He blinked them back, refusing to let them fall. Cowboys didn't cry, no matter how much it hurt.

Saying nothing, Roxanne placed her hand over the back of his. Without a word, Tom turned his palm up, twined his fingers with hers, and held on tight.

Two and a half hours later, the surgeon stepped into the waiting room. Tom shot to his feet, dragging Roxanne with him, jostling Augie who sat up and blinked like a sleepy toddler.

"He came through like a champ," the doctor said, answering the question before anyone could ask it. "And no, you can't see him yet," he added, anticipating the next one. "He's still in recovery. He's going to be there for the next little while, until the anesthesia wears off, then we'll take him back to his room. You could probably see him for a few minutes then, but he's still going to be mostly out of it and won't remember whether you were there of not. I'd suggest you all go on home, get some sleep your-

selves and come back tonight after supper. He'll be
ready for company then.''

SEVERAL MILES from the hospital, they turned off the
two-lane blacktop onto a long graveled road that was
marked only by the tall, gateless arch that spanned its
width. The top of the arch bore the same insignia—
the Roman numeral II superimposed over a capital
C—that decorated the side of the blue pickup. At the
end of the road, a quarter mile distance or more, as
far as Roxanne could tell, was a copse of trees and
what appeared to be several buildings. As they neared
the end of the road, Roxanne was able to make out a
barn—the largest of the structures—and two smaller
buildings, perhaps a bunkhouse and a henhouse or
toolshed, she thought. They were set to the side and
slightly behind the stand of cottonwoods and oaks that
sheltered the ranch house itself.

It was weathered old Victorian, white clapboard
with slate-blue shutters. A wide covered porch
wrapped around the entire first level. There were dormer windows on the third level—the attic, Roxanne
decided—and a pair of rocking chairs on the porch on
either side of the front door. A small picket fence
enclosed the front door and one side of the house,
protecting a struggling green patch of lawn and a
thriving vegetable garden from rambunctious boys
and livestock. Roxanne thought it could have used a
few touches, a new coat of paint on the front door
and shutters, some colorful hanging plants on the
porch, maybe a flowerbed to soften the foundation,

but all in all, it was warm, inviting and utterly charming.

"By Texas standards, it's not all that big a spread," Tom said as they got out of the truck. "But it's home."

It was also as chaotic as Tom had predicted it would be. Nearly a dozen young boys, from ages six to sixteen, came running toward the truck as it rolled down the long driveway and came to a stop in the yard between the gleaming forest-green pickup and the late-model Chevy sedan that sat in the driveway next to the house. All of them were talking a mile a minute, all of them were clamoring for news and attention. The littlest one, tears running down his face, attached himself to Tom's legs and demanded to know if it was true that the Padre was dead.

Tom stooped, snagging the child under his rear end with one arm, and lifted him on to his hip. Placing the thumb and index finger of his free hand against his front teeth, he gave a piercing whistle to settle the rest of them down.

"The Padre is going to be fine," he said into the ensuing silence. "The by-pass operation is over and the doctor said he's resting comfortably."

"Does that mean he's not dead?" blubbered the little boy.

"Yes, Petie, that means he's not dead." He wiped at the little child's cheek with the pad of his thumb in a gesture so natural and tender it made Roxanne's heart turn over in her chest. "After supper tonight, I'll take you to the hospital so you can see for yourself, okay?"

"Can we go, too?" said one of the other boys.

"Not everybody all at once." Tom bent to set Petie back on his own two feet. "That'd be too much for him to handle just yet, and the hospital wouldn't allow so many visitors at one time, anyway. We'll have to go in shifts. A few tonight, a few tomorrow morning, a few more tomorrow night, and so on until it's time for him to come home, That way, we won't tire him out and he'll have plenty of visitors to look forward to while he's there."

"How long's he gonna be there?" another child wanted to know.

"Yeah, Tom, when's he comin' home?"

"He'll be home in a week. Maybe less if he heals up real fast." He swept his gaze over the anxious, eager faces upturned to his, looking for one in particular. "Where's Jared?" he said, when he didn't find it.

"Right here." A young teenager, barely into puberty, stepped away from the rear fender of the pickup where he had been loitering, just outside the circle. Unlike the other boys, who wore cowboy boots and trim Western-cut shirts neatly tucked into their jeans, Jared sported a long-billed baseball cap and a baggy, too large T-shirt that hung over a pair of camouflage pants. His boots looked as if he'd picked them up at an army surplus outlet. He had a little silver ring dangling from the outside corner of his right eyebrow and his attitude was such that Roxanne wouldn't have been surprised to see him put a cigarette between his lips and light it while they watched. She remembered that Augie had referred to him as "the new kid."

Tom smiled and moved toward him through the crowd of kids. "I understand we owe you a real debt of gratitude," he said, and extended his hand.

The boy took it automatically. "Huh?"

"Augie tells me that it's due to your quick thinking that we still have the Padre with us today."

"Huh?"

"I what?" said Augie.

"You're the one who insisted on calling 9-1-1 when the Padre collapsed, aren't you?"

"Well, yeah. Sure." The boy shrugged. "I guess."

"Then you're the hero of the hour," Tom told him. "The surgeon said that if the paramedics had gotten to the Padre even a few minutes later, he probably wouldn't have made it. You saved his life."

"I did?"

"He did?" said Augie.

"You did," Tom said. "And we all owe you our thanks." His steely blue gaze touched each boy in turn. "Don't we?"

Petie, the youngest and most unselfconscious member of the little group, stepped forward and threw his skinny arms around Jared's waist in a show of unfettered appreciation. "Thank you, Jared," he said. "Thankyouthankyouthankyou."

Looking slightly panic-stricken, Jared patted the little boy's shoulder awkwardly. "You're welcome, Petie."

That made the other boys laugh in commiseration— they'd all been the focus of Petie's unbridled enthusiasm at one time or another—and they surged forward, each eager to shake Jared's hand. Tom let the congratulations go on for a few minutes, then stepped into the fray before the backslapping and handshakes could descend into roughhousing.

"Don't you all have chores that need doing?" he said, neatly dispersing them.

"That," Roxanne said, smiling up into his face as the boys hurried off in various directions, "was absolutely masterful. I am in complete and utter awe. You must be a wonderful teacher."

He shrugged, looking as uneasy as young Jared had a few moments before. "It weren't nothin', ma'am," he said, parodying both the accent and attitude of the stereotypical bashful cowboy to hide his own embarrassment at her praise.

"Is she your girlfriend?"

They turned as one to find Petie staring up at them.

"Don't you have chores?" Tom said.

"I already finished feeding the chickens, and I pulled the weeds, too. Is she?"

"Is she what?" Tom said, stalling.

"Is she your girlfriend?'

"Well…" He shot a quick glance at Roxanne to see how she was taking the question. His gut instinct was to answer in the affirmative, but he didn't know how she would feel about that. *Was* she his girlfriend. Did that describe what they were to each other? Or did the word "girlfriend" imply a level of commitment they didn't share?

She looked back at him, her expression bland and noncommittal, waiting to hear what he would say.

"Well…" Tom said again, having found no help there. "She's a girl and she's my friend."

"Tom has a girlfriend. Tom has a girlfriend," Petie screeched, and went running off to tell the other boys.

Tom's gaze went back to Roxanne's face. "Should I have told him something else?"

"I don't know what it would be," she said. "I don't think there's actually a word for what we are to each other." The thought that there wasn't tugged uncomfortably at her heartstrings. The lack of a word to describe their relationship made them seem so…temporary. Which they were, of course, but… She shrugged to show it didn't matter one way or the other. "Girlfriend works for me if it works for you."

"It works for me,' he said, his voice and demeanor just as carefully casual as hers had been. He reached out, putting his hand on the small of her back. "Let's get inside. I need to make a couple of phone calls, let Rooster know how things are going," he said, as he ushered her up the wide steps of the ranch house to the wraparound porch. "I probably ought to call Miz Jensen, too, and—"

"Would that be Jo Beth Jensen?" Roxanne said with an arch look.

He grinned. "No, that'd be her mama. She's the one who always gets called when someone here 'bouts needs a neighborly hand. I need to call and let her know I'm here so's she doesn't have to be inconvenienced any more than necessary. Then we'll get you settled in and—"

There was a young woman standing at the old-fashioned white enamel sink with a plastic ice cube tray in her hands. She was curvy and petite with long, soft brown hair clipped back at the nape of her neck, and big soft brown eyes. She was wearing an apron over her jeans and nice sensible brown leather cowboy boots with modestly high heels. Her blouse was pale pink, with a narrow row of twining leaves and flowers outlining the Western-cut yoke. There was a pot of something savory simmering on the big six-burner stove, and three fruit pies cooling on trivets on the long wooden kitchen table.

Roxanne suddenly felt like something the cat had dragged in off the street. She'd managed to slip into a bathroom at the hospital and take a few minutes to freshen up, finger-combing her hair into some kind of order and applying a fresh coat of cherry-red lipstick, but she was still wearing the same clothes she'd been wearing all night—the snug red tank top and tight jeans, the high-heeled red boots. Tom's jacket was still slung over her shoulders. She resisted the urge to pull it together in front so she could hide behind it.

"I thought that must be you when I heard the truck pull up outside," the other woman said, smiling at Tom. "I would have been right out, but I had to take my pies out of the oven before they burned. And then I thought I might as well just take a minute and make some more iced tea." She dumped the ice cubes into a glass pitcher as she spoke. "The boys drank the last of it with their dinner and I know how you like your iced tea when you've been outside in the heat." She set the empty ice cube tray in the sink and dried her hands on her apron. "Hello," she said, extending her hand to Roxanne as she crossed the width of the kitchen. "I'm Jo Beth. Jo Beth Jensen. And you are…?"

11

Tom introduced her to Jo Beth as his friend. Not his girlfriend, which they'd both just agreed was as good a designation as any, but simply as his *friend.* He removed his hand from the small of her back and got all distant and formal and tongue-tied—which she knew damn well he wasn't!—and acted as if they were nothing more to each other than mere acquaintances. Casual ones, at that.

Jo Beth was no dummy, of course; Tom wouldn't have considered marrying a stupid woman. She knew something was up, that there was more to their relationship than he was letting on, but she was too polite—or too crafty—to make an issue of it. Instead, she delivered a few instructions about last-minute touches to the pot of chili that was simmering on the stove—"Should I write this down or do you think you can remember it?" she said sweetly to Roxanne—and removed her apron.

"Will you look at the time," she said, as she headed toward the door. "I told Dad I'd be home by three and it's nearly that already. He wants me to go with him to take a look at some breeding stock Matt Thomas—you know, the T Bar ranch just this side of Vashti?—has for sale. He's probably pacing up and

down the front porch by now, cussing me out something fierce.'' She laughed lightly, as if the threat of
being cussed out by her father was more amusing than
anything else, and went up on tiptoe to plant a quick,
friendly kiss on Tom's cheek.

He stood, stiff and uncomfortable and indisputably
guilty, his hands at his sides, and didn't kiss her back.

She didn't seem to notice his lack of response.

''Tell the Padre that Mom and I will be over to see
him in the next couple of days, hear? We'll sneak him
in a piece of cherry pie.'' She held her hand out to
Roxanne again. ''It was very nice to meet you,'' she
said pleasantly, although it was patently clear—to
Roxanne, at least—that it was nothing of the kind.
''Do you think you'll be able to stay long enough for
the party?''

''Party?''

''Oh, nothing like you're probably used to,'' she
trilled, somehow making it seem as if the parties Roxanne was probably used to were along the line of
drunken orgies. ''Nothing fancy. It'll just be a quiet,
neighborly little get-together to celebrate when the Padre comes home from the hospital. Like the one we
had for Dad—remember?'' she looked up at Tom
''—after he had *his* by-pass two years ago. And don't
worry—'' she patted him on the shoulder ''—you
don't have to do a thing. Mom and I have already got
everything all planned except for the date.'' The
screen door squeaked in protest as she opened it.
''You ought to squirt a little WD-40 on that before it
gets worse,'' she said, and then the door closed gently

behind her—she didn't slam it the way Roxanne wanted to—and she was gone.

Tom and Roxanne stood silently, not looking at each other, listening as Jo Beth started up the engine of the shiny green truck—not revving it the way Roxanne would have—made a Y-turn in the graveled yard, and drove sedately away.

"So. That's little miss Texas A&M with the degree in animal science. Rooster was right. She's very pretty." Roxanne picked up the spoon sitting neatly in the spoon rest on the kitchen counter and dipped it into the pot on the stove. "And she makes great chili, too. I can certainly see why you're thinking of marrying her."

"For the last time, I am *not* thinking of marrying her," he said. And it was the absolute truth. He wasn't thinking of marrying her. Not seriously. Not anymore.

"Really?" The spoon still clutched in her hand, Roxanne turned around to face him. "Well—" She leaned back against the counter, folded her arms over her chest, and crossed one booted ankle over the other. "You'd better start running, then, because she's certainly thinking of marrying you, sugar."

ROXANNE TOLD HERSELF that if she had any pride or self-respect, she'd have left the Second Chance right after Jo Beth did. She'd have demanded the keys to that rattletrap old pickup parked out in the yard, driven herself to the municipal airport and gotten on a plane for Dallas. Instead, there she was, tucked up in one of a narrow pair of twin beds in an attic room with steeply slanted ceilings and a single dormer window overlooking what appeared to be the north forty. The walls were painted pale green, the floors were hardwood, the bedspreads were patchwork quilts, the furniture was rich golden oak, and the bedsteads were painted white iron.

And she was lying in one of them, dressed in nothing but her leopard-print underwear and a dab of Passion behind each knee, waiting for all the kids to go to sleep so Tom could sneak up and join her. She'd obviously become a slave to her hormones. Or a slave to his, she wasn't sure which.

She'd been about to throw the chili spoon at his head—she'd had her hand cocked back, ready to let fly—when he'd started across the room in that slow deliberate way he had, moving with that loose-kneed, hip-rolling, purposeful cowboy swagger of his that always made her mouth water, and curled his fingers around her wrist.

"I swear to God, Slim. There's nothing between Jo Beth and me. I've never given her *any* reason to think there was," he said earnestly.

And then he kissed her. He didn't lean into her, or grind his pelvis against hers. He didn't let his hands wander to her breasts or her butt or between her legs. He just kissed her.

Completely.

Thoroughly.

At length.

Lips and tongue and teeth, all nibbling and licking and nipping at hers, making hot, sweet love to her mouth with nothing but his mouth, the way he had that last night in Cheyenne. She gave in to it without a murmur of protest, coiling her arms around him like a lariat when he let go of her wrist to cup her head and tilt it to a better angle. They didn't break apart until the screen door screeched on its hinges and half a dozen boys of various sizes and shapes trampled into the kitchen like a herd of rambunctious young cattle.

"Tom has a girlfriend. Tom has a girlfriend," little Petie singsonged, making Roxanne wonder if he'd been chanting the words ever since Tom sent him chasing off after the other boys.

Jared hooked an arm around the smaller boy's neck. "Give it a rest, kid," he said, and slapped his hand over Petie's mouth.

A brief tussle ensued, ending with Petie giggling delightedly as he dangled upside down over his new best friend's shoulder. His new best friend, Roxanne noted, who was wearing a battered black cowboy hat in place of his baseball cap. She glanced at Tom to see if he'd noticed. His secret smile of satisfaction told her he had.

"I brought your gear in," said Augie, the responsible one, as he hefted the two bags up on the end of the table. "Where do you want me to put hers?"

"Please don't bother putting it anywhere," Roxanne said, mindful that the boy still regarded her with suspicion. "I can take it myself, if you'll just tell me where."

"We use the dormer room for guests," Augie said. "It's all the way at the top of the stairs. In the attic."

"It's small, but it's private," Tom added, "and you've got your own bathroom up there."

"We came in to get something to eat," one of the smaller boys said, tired of all the adult chitchat.

All eyes turned to the three pies cooling on the table.

"After dinner," Tom said, before they could ask. "If you're hungry now, have an apple." He grabbed one out of the big wooden bowl sitting on the tiled kitchen counter and led by example, biting into the crisp green Granny Smith. "We'll be out in the barn." He dropped a quick kiss on Roxanne's lips. "Holler if you need any help figuring out Jo Beth's instructions about the chili," he said, and pushed open the creaky screen door.

Roxanne *would* have thrown the spoon at him then, except that there were children present and she didn't want to set a bad example. Instead, she stirred the chili and contented herself with a hidden smirk over the smear of chili sauce he wore across the back of his shirt.

She carried her bag upstairs to the dormer room tucked up under the eaves and unpacked, shaking out her clothing and hanging it up in the lovely old-fashioned armoire that graced nearly the whole of one wall. She tidied up in the tiny but nicely appointed connecting bathroom, then headed back downstairs to the kitchen.

Since she didn't have anything else to do, anyway, and nothing else to occupy her time, she prepared a large tray of crudités and rolled out a mammoth batch of fluffy made-from-scratch biscuits just to prove that little miss Texas A&M wasn't the only one who could cook. Not that she hadn't proved it already—and quite well, too, she thought—but grilled chicken breasts and salads were a far cry from chili and cherry pies, especially with a bunch of boys. She considered dropping the pies on the floor and calling it an accident, but good sense prevailed when she realized she had neither the time nor the ingredients necessary to whip up one of her famous chocolate-fudge cheesecakes to replace them.

It was then, when she caught herself wondering if chocolate-fudge cheesecake would tip the balance in her favor and make him fall in love with her, that she realized there was no *probably* about getting her heart broken. It was going to happen. It was only a matter of timing. Now, or six weeks from now, it was going to happen.

And *that's* when she should have headed out to the truck and taken off for the airport.

Instead, she was lying in a strange bed under the eaves, listening for the telltale creak of the attic stairs and wondering just how long it took a dozen young boys to fall asleep.

TOM WAS BEGINNING to think the boys would *never* get to sleep. Lord knew, they should all be dead tired. He certainly was. Or would be, if he weren't looking forward to creeping upstairs to the attic bedroom. After supper, he'd taken Petie and two of the other boys to the hospital with him to see the Padre. It had been an emotionally charged experience, with Petie starting in to cry as soon as he saw the Padre in the hospital bed, hooked up to all the various drains and IVs, looking frail and bruised and sick. The other two boys, being nine and eleven respectively, had struggled manfully against their own tears and managed to keep them to a few discreet sniffles, wiped off on their shirtsleeves when they thought no one was looking. Tom wished he'd been blessed with Petie's lack of inhibitions; he would have liked to howl, too, and let the nurse carry him off to get a soda pop out of the vending machine at the end of the hallway.

Instead, he waited until the other two boys trailed Petie and the nurse out into the hall and put his hand over the frail veined one laying so quietly against the sheets and squeezed gently. "How you feeling, Padre?"

"I feel like I've been kicked in the chest by a bad-tempered bronc," the old man grumbled. "How the hell else would I feel?"

Tom felt the tight knot of tension inside him give way. Despite the hospital bed and the tubes and the monitoring machines, the Padre was the same irascible, indomitable, straight-from-the-cuff kind of man he had always been. "You gave everybody quite a scare," Tom said.

"I gave myself quite a scare," the Padre admitted. "Thought for sure I was a goner. If it hadn't been for Jared, yelling for somebody to call 9-1-1, I would have been. You be sure to let the rest of them know I said that, you hear? They've been riding him pretty hard these past few months. Testing the new kid out, just like they always do. Not that he doesn't give it back to them, just as hard as they dish it out, but I've thought for sure, a couple of times, that he was going to rabbit on us. I wouldn't like to lose him."

"I don't think you have to worry about that anymore. Before supper tonight, he was ridin' Petie on his shoulder and wearing Augie's old black hat."

"Oh, that's good. That's real good. He's a good kid, deep down. He's got real potential."

"You think they've all got potential."

"And they all do," he said, with utter conviction. "You've just got to help them find it."

Petie came back into the room then, trailed by the other two boys. He seemed to have regained his equilibrium, and came right up to the edge of the bed, more curious than scared now. "Tom's got a girlfriend," he said, wanting to be the first to impart the news.

"Does he now?" The Padre slanted a glance at Tom. "What's her name?" he asked Petie.

"Roxy."

"Roxy, huh? Is that a new one?"

"Well, I ain't never seen her around before."

"Haven't ever," Tom corrected automatically.

"I haven't ever seen her around before," Petie repeated obediently. "She's kinda skinny, but I like her hair. It's the same color as Goldie's tail." Goldie was a gentle old palomino mare all the Second Chance kids learned to ride on. "And she makes real good biscuits. I had about ten of 'em." He took a sip of his soda pop. "Tom was kissin' her in the kitchen before supper."

The Padre uttered a bark of delighted laughter. It ended in a wheezing cough that had him grasping his chest. "I'm all right," he said, waving Tom back down when he jumped up to summon the nurse. "I'm all right, damn it. It just hurts when I laugh, is all."

Tom summoned the nurse, anyway.

"I think you've had just about enough visiting for tonight, Padre," she said severely. "Say good-night to your guests and we'll get you ready for bed."

"I'll say good-night when I'm damned good and ready to say good-night," he groused, "and not a damned minute sooner." He motioned for Tom to lean closer. "This new girl of yours with the palomino hair, she wouldn't happen to be the little firecracker Rooster told me about, would she?"

"I don't know," Tom hedged. "What did Rooster tell you?"

"Only that you were so smitten you couldn't see straight," he said, and began to wheeze again at the expression on Tom's face. "You bring her to see me, you hear?" he ordered, clutching his chest with one hand and waving the nurse off with the other. "I want to get a look at her."

The nurse stood firm and shooed them all out into the hall.

And now Tom had a word for his feelings about Roxanne. He was smitten, that was all. Besotted. Infatuated. Perhaps even a little bit obsessed. But he was not, thank God, in love. Not love with a capital L, anyway.

SHE WAS ASLEEP when he finally judged it safe to sneak up the stairs. She lay on her side on top of the covers on the narrow bed, in her ridiculously sexy underwear, with her knees drawn up like a child and her hands tucked under her cheek. The bedside lamp cast exotic shadows over her face, giving her a look of mystery that was excitingly at odds with the prim, little-girl position of her body. The ceiling fan turned lazily overhead, causing just enough air movement to ruffle the edges of her tangled blond mop. She was adorable and sexy and inexplicably dear.

He tiptoed across the room, meaning only to turn out the light she'd left on and kiss her good-night before creeping back down the stairs to his own bed, but her eyelids fluttered open at the butterfly brush of his lips against her cheek.

"Hey, cowboy," she whispered, and smiled at him.

"Hey, Slim" he said, and nuzzled her nose with his.

Their lips met briefly, parted, then met again and clung. Without breaking the second kiss, he stretched out beside her and took her into his arms. Their loving was sweet and slow and careful, there on the narrow bed in the tiny attic room, both of them more than a little tired and mindful of the need for discretion with a houseful of children sleeping in the rooms below them. There was no frantic writhing or muffled screams or graphic words of lustful encouragement and appreciation. Instead there were soft rustlings, and softer sighs and softly murmured words. When it was over and contentment had mellowed them both and soothed the jagged edges of the day, he turned her onto her side and spooned her from behind, cuddling her close to his heart.

"Did I remember to thank you for dinner?" he whispered into her hair.

"Yes." She yawned. "I believe you did."

"I was only teasing you about the chili, you know. I didn't actually expect you to go ahead and make supper for all those kids."

"Yes, I know," she said, which was partially— okay, mostly—why she'd done it. To show him that anything Jo Beth could do, she could do better. Or just as well, anyway.

"Those biscuits were the best I've ever tasted. The boys liked them, too. Petie told the Padre he ate ten of them."

"It weren't nothin'," she drawled modestly, feeling the warm glow of his praise wash over her.

She felt his chest move as he chuckled against her back. "You could have knocked me over with a feather when I walked in the kitchen and saw those two huge plates of biscuits setting on the table next to Jo Beth's chili. I'd never have pegged you as the down-home domestic type if I hadn't seen it with my own eyes."

"Oh, really?" She felt the warm glow fade a little, wondering if he'd suddenly forgotten all those meals she'd cooked on the road the past couple of weeks. Didn't that count as domestic? Or were grilled chicken and salads lower on the domesticity scale than chili and cherry pie? "What type do you have me pegged as?"

"Oh—" she felt him skim a hand through her hair, lifting it away from her head and letting it fall back "—one of those pampered trust-fund babies, I guess," he said, basing his assessment on her effort-less high-tone polish even in bright-red boots and skintight jeans, and a vaguely remembered mention of a stock portfolio and household staff. "The kind born with a silver spoon in her mouth, with servants to do the cooking and cleaning. And no need for you to do anything except collect your stock dividends and have a good time."

The warm glow turned into a cold lump in the middle of her chest. Was that really what he thought of her? That she was some useless parasite who spent her life partying? And wasn't that *exactly* what she'd intended him to think when she picked him up at Ed Earl's? That she was a carefree, fast-living, good-time girl? Talk about being hoist on your own petard! She'd played the role so well, he couldn't see through it to the real her.

"Am I close?" he probed, hoping she'd tell him he was way off base, hoping she would say that the woman who'd scolded them about their lousy eating habits, and did their laundry with hers, and read to them on the road was the real her. That the woman who'd competently and cheerfully made dinner for a dozen hungry boys was who she really was under the high-tone polish and sexy exterior.

That woman might actually want to stay and make a life with him on the Second Chance; the trust-fund baby would be gone in six weeks, eager to get back to her life of ease and privilege.

Roxanne knew she could tell him he was wrong, of course. Except that he wasn't, completely. The picture he painted was just true enough—except for the partying part—that she wasn't able to deny it. "Close enough," she said, and managed an insouciant little laugh to cover her dismay.

She felt him sigh against her neck, and then, a moment later, he raised himself up on an elbow and leaned over her shoulder. "I'd better get out of here before I fall asleep and blow our cover." He kissed her cheek and slipped out of bed, heading down the stairs to greet the dawn in his own room.

Roxanne lay there after he had gone, staring at the moonlight shining in through the dormer window, and wondered why her heart felt as if it had already started to crack.

"DO WE HAVE TO do this *now?*" Roxanne asked, sounding, even to her own ears, like a whiny little kid. She tried to inject a little adult rationality into her voice. "I mean, really, wouldn't it be better to wait until he's out of the hospital?"

She'd already decided—*almost*—that she'd be gone by then. It would be much better to leave now, before the summer was over, rather than drag it out for the remaining few weeks. They could end it on a high note, leaving each other with happy memories of hot sex, good times, and lots of laughter. If she stayed much longer, she had a sneaking suspicion it would end in tears. On her part, anyway. And that would be a damned undignified end to her Wild West adventure.

"A string of visitors all day long can't be good for a man who's just had a triple by-pass," she said. "And I'm sure he'd rather see one of the boys instead of me, anyway."

"He asked me specifically to bring you in for a visit."

"He *asked* to see me?"

"Actually, it was more of an order." Tom slanted a quick glance at her as he maneuvered the pickup into an empty spot in the parking lot. "He said he wants to get a look at you."

"Get a look at me?" She got a hunted look in her eyes. "Why?"

He grinned evilly, but she was too agitated to notice. "Said he wanted to make sure I hadn't introduced his boys to some loose woman who'd exert a corrupting influence on their developing psyches."

"I'd say it's probably too late to be worried about that, since we've already been introduced," Roxanne said. The words were nonchalant, but her palms were sweating.

She had a pretty good idea of what the Padre would see when he looked at her. Tight jeans, red boots, a snug little eyelet camisole top with too much cleavage showing for the middle of the day, topped by a deliberately tangled mop of flyaway blond hair. And the nails, she thought, catching sight of them as she rubbed her damp palms up and down her jeans-covered thighs. Let's not forget the man-killer nails. He was going to think she was some kind of Jezebel, for sure.

"You scared?" Tom said.

"Scared? Me?" She lifted her chin. "Of course not."

But she was. Scared to death. She'd built up an image of him in her mind. This saintly man they all

called the Padre. This selfless paragon of virtue who
had studied for the priesthood, then gave it up to min-
ister to lost boys instead. She kept picturing someone
like the late Spencer Tracy in his priestly garb in the
movie *Boys Town* or, even scarier, Charlton Heston
in any one of his biblical epics, stern and condemning
and regal.

Instead, she found a grizzled old lion of a man in
a faded green hospital gown, a little plastic bracelet
around his left wrist. His hair was thick and dark,
heavily sprinkled with gray. His face was brown and
leathered with age, sagging a bit at the jowls, but still
strong and craggily handsome in a patriarchal kind of
way. He looked a little tired, a little frail, even to
someone like Roxanne, who was unfamiliar with his
normal appearance. He was leaning back against the
sharply elevated head of the hospital bed, drinking a
Dr Pepper through a straw, and carrying on a quiet
conversation with a very attractive woman sitting in
the visitor's chair in front of the window.

Tom checked in the doorway, as if in surprise, then
dropped Roxanne's hand and hurried forward. "Hello,
Mom," he said, bending down to kiss the woman's
smooth cheek. "I didn't realize you were in town.
How are you?"

Mom? This lovely, soft-eyed woman, who didn't
look more than forty years old, was Tom's mother?
What kind of setup was this? Not only was she going
to meet the man who was, to all intents and purposes,
her lover's father, but now she had to face his mother,
too? Was she being checked out? Roxanne wondered,
resisting the urge to tug the front of her camisole a

little higher on her chest. Were they going to gang up and warn her away before she could corrupt their darling boy? She lifted her chin, determined to brazen it out.

And rather enjoying the prospect, too, she realized. She'd never been warned away before. It made her feel like a dangerous woman. She'd never felt like a dangerous woman before. It was kind of exhilarating.

"I had no idea what had happened until Hector called me himself last night," Tom's mother was saying plaintively. "I wish someone had thought to let me know sooner." She looked up at Tom, her expression gently reproachful. "I would have gotten one of other nurses to take my shift at the hospital and come immediately."

"Now, now, Molly, don't fret," soothed the Padre. "There was no need for you to be here any sooner. There was nothing you could have done, except sit around and wait like everyone else. It's much better that you're here now, so we can visit. And isn't it nice that Tom's brought his new friend so you get a chance to meet her, too?"

He turned suddenly, his gaze pinning Roxanne where she stood, still hovering in the doorway. His eyes were brown and alive and knowing. His teeth, when he smiled at her, were strong and white, more than capable of taking a bite out of anything that got in his way.

"Come on over here, girl," he said, and held out his hand, motioning her forward with an imperious flick of his fingers, reminding her, suddenly, of Charlton Heston at his most imposing biblical best. This man, too, could have parted the Red Sea with a flick of his hand, even lying on his back in a hospital bed. "Let's have a look at you."

Roxanne crossed the room and put her hand in his. His grip was warm and firm. "Well, introduce us," he said to Tom, without taking his eyes off Roxanne.

She held his gaze steadily, without flinching, the same way she'd held Tom's at Ed Earl's in Lubbock. Her chin was elevated, her eyes full of silent challenge and bravado. No way were they going to see her sweat.

The Padre chuckled approvingly.

Tom couldn't hide the surge of pride he felt. "Mom. Padre. I'd like you both to meet Roxy Archer. Roxy, this is my mother, Molly Steele. And this—" the pride showed through, here, too "—is Hector Menendez. Better known as the Padre."

"Ms. Steele," Roxanne said crisply, dipping her head in her best finishing school fashion, as if she were standing there clad in a demure linen shift and graduated pearls instead of blue jeans and dusty red boots. "Mr. Menendez. A pleasure to meet you both."

"No need to stand on ceremony with me, girl. You can call me Padre like everybody else does around here. Sit yourself down—" he tugged on her hand "—right there on the edge of the bed is fine. You won't hurt me—and tell us about yourself. Tom, here, has been pretty scant on the details. How'd you two meet?"

Roxanne flicked a glance at Tom, silently asking for directions.

He smiled back blandly, leaving it up to her.

"I picked him up in Ed Earl's Polynesian Dance Palace in Lubbock after the rodeo," she said, letting them make of it what they would.

Molly Steele pursed her lips disapprovingly.

The Padre looked as if he were turning over her answer in his mind, reserving judgment until he knew more.

"Anything else you'd like to know?" she said to him, with the air of a smart-ass child pretending to be helpful.

"Well—" his dark eyes twinkled "—what do you do with yourself when you're not chasing cowboys?"

Tom smothered a laugh.

"Hector, really! What kind of a question is that?" chided Tom's mother.

"It's a perfectly legitimate question. I want to know what she does. Girl's a grown woman. She must have something that keeps her busy. She can't chase cowboys all day, can she?"

"I'm a teacher," Roxanne said.

"A *teacher!*" That was Tom, expressing his surprise.

"And for the record," she said, ignoring him in favor of addressing her remarks to the man in the hospital bed. "I've only chased one cowboy." She paused for effect. "So far," she said, and batted her lashes flirtatiously, blatantly intimating that she might be persuaded to broaden her horizons for him.

The Padre wheezed out what lately passed for his version of a laugh. "Girl's a real firecracker," he said, slapping his knee through the bedclothes. "Just like Rooster said."

"Where do you teach?" Tom said quietly, drawing her attention back to him.

"St. Catherine's Academy in Stamford, Connecticut. It's a fully accredited private school," she said, in case he doubted it. "Kindergarten through twelfth, both boarders and day students. I teach fifth grade English Lit and Latin."

"That where you're from?" the Padre asked. "Connecticut?"

"Born and raised."

"Got family there?"

"My parents and three brothers. One older and two younger," she said before he could ask. "A sister-in-law and two nieces, with another on the way."

"Any beaus?"

"Dozens," she lied.

"Then what in blazes are you doing down here in Texas?"

"Why, I thought you knew—" she slipped into her cornpone-and-molasses accent "—I'm down here chasin' cowboys on my summer vacation." She batted her eyelashes again, tilting her chin down so she could look up at him through her lashes. "You interested, sugar?"

The Padre wheezed delightedly.

ROXANNE WAITED until she and Tom were in the truck and on their way back to the Second Chance before she pounced. "Well, that was a nice little ambush you arranged."

Tom cast a wary glance at her out of the corner of his eye. "Ambush?"

"You didn't tell me your mother was going to be there."

"Because I didn't know she was going to be there."

Roxanne uttered an inelegant little snort. "Uh-huh."

"I swear, it was as much a surprise to me as it was to you. The last time my mother was in Bowie was when I had that concussion a year ago last May."

"Are you saying she only comes to visit when someone is sick?"

"Yeah, I guess that about sums it up," Tom conceded. "Since she left, nothing much less than a medical emergency will get her to set foot in Bowie."

"Not your birthday? Thanksgiving? Christmas?"

"Oh, my birthday, sure, when I was a kid. And holidays, too, sometimes, when she could get off work. After I got old enough to drive, though, I'd usually go to Dallas to see her. It's easier on everybody that way."

"Everybody who?"

"My mother, mostly," he admitted. "Bowie doesn't have a lot of good memories for her."

"It has you," she said, beginning to form a very poor opinion of Tom's mother.

It was one thing to turn him over to the care of someone who could do a better job of raising him. It was quite another to abandon him entirely to that someone else's care, even if that someone was the Padre. A child needed to know his mother loved him.

Tom took his eyes off the road a minute to look at her. "Don't make it into something tragic, Slim. It isn't. She did what she had to do, for her and for me, and we're both okay with that. She just hates it here, is all." He reached over and patted her thigh. "And I'm okay with that, too."

"I'll tell you something else she hates," Roxanne said. "Me."

He flicked another glance at her. "What makes you say a thing like that?"

"Oh, please." Roxanne rolled her eyes. "She thinks I'm a loose woman out to snag her baby boy and she doesn't like it—or me—one little bit."

Tom shook his head. "You must have misunderstood something she said."

"Oh, it wasn't anything she *said.* Not directly. It was more the way she looked at me. As if I had just strolled in off of the street."

He reached sideways and placed his palm on her forehead. "You feverish?"

"I'm serious." She grabbed his hand between both of hers. "Your mother thinks I'm going to corrupt you. So—" she brought his hand to her mouth and sucked his index finger inside, and pulled it out, very slowly "—how am I doing?" she said, and grinned at him.

12

TWO DAYS LATER—fully three days ahead of schedule and against his doctor's advice—the Padre checked himself out of the hospital and demanded to be taken home. Tom agreed to the plan only if a nurse came with him and stayed for what would have been the remaining three days of a standard hospital stay for a triple by-pass patient. The Padre grumbled, declaring his boys could provide all the care he needed, but Tom was adamant and the nurse and her equipment were bundled into the truck for the ride to Second Chance.

And Roxanne, against all her better judgment and the resolutions she made in the middle of the night after Tom left her to sneak back to his own bed before the boys woke up, was still there. Since it would be churlish to leave before the Padre's welcome home party—planned for three days hence, when he would have returned to the Second Chance had he been inclined to follow doctor's orders—she decided to stay for just that much longer. Besides, Rooster would be there for the party, too, flush with his success in Cheyenne and Wichita and Oklahoma City, and she wanted to say goodbye to him before she left. They'd gotten to be good friends on those long rides between rodeos. She owed him a personal goodbye.

But then she was absolutely, definitely, without a doubt, leaving.

She'd gotten what she came for, after all. She'd found her good-looking dangerous cowboy and had her Wild West adventure. It was time to bow out, to retreat with good grace, while the Welcome mat was still out. She didn't want to wait around until the end, to see him wondering when she was going to pack up and go so he could get on with the nice little life he had planned for himself. She didn't want to wait until he had—God forbid—"gotten his fill of her." She wanted to leave while she could still see the want in his eyes, while that nice little life full of kids and cows—and the wife, let's not forget the wife, she told herself sternly—was still only something he was thinking about as a part of his future.

She wasn't going to be heart-whole when she left— any possibility of that had disappeared somewhere on the road between one rodeo and the next—but she was going to go in style, with her head held high and her dignity intact.

It helped, a little, that the only place for the Padre's nurse to bunk while she was at the Second Chance was up in the little attic room with Roxanne. It cut down considerably on the opportunity for her to dissolve into undignified tears and declare her undying love to a man who, by no stretch of her imagination, wanted to hear those words from the woman who was his "last fling."

She'd come dangerously close a couple of times,

up in that little attic room in the middle of the night. The sex was sweeter between them in that room, more gentle and tender. Maybe it was the narrow bed, which limited their more wild sexual antics, or the need to be quiet so as not to alert the boys to what was going on over their heads. Maybe it was the fact that he got up and left her when the loving was over that made her want to cling and cry. Whatever it was, the room was dangerous.

Since the nurse had been sharing it with her, though, they'd had to rely on quickies at odd times and out-of-the-way places, which neatly precluded the trappings of romance that weakened her resolve. Roxanne had approached the lack of privacy with a positive attitude, seeing it as both safeguard against embarrassing confessions and an opportunity to fulfill as many of her remaining sexual fantasies as possible and store up memories for what was sure to be the coming sexual drought.

"WAIT, WAIT—" she was panting and wet, her jeans and panties on the floor of the truck, her blouse and bra pushed up around her neck, trying to maneuver so she could straddle his lap "—the steering wheel is in the way."

Without removing his mouth from her breast, he shifted position, edging over into the passenger side of the cab, and cupped his hands around the backs of her bare thighs to guide her legs to either side of his.

"Now the gearshift is in the way," she moaned.

"That's not the gearshift," he said, and slid into her.

"STOP IT!" She giggled and slapped at his hands, trying to wriggle away as he burrowed down the front of her jeans. Since he had her pressed up against the wall in the tack room, she couldn't wriggle very far. And she wasn't trying very hard. "Stop it right now," she said again, sucking in her stomach to make it easier for him to find what he was searching for. "I think someone's coming."

"That'd be you," he said, as he found the swollen little nubbin between her legs and began to massage it.

"GOOD GOD ALMIGHTY, woman! You're going to get us killed."

She raised her head from his lap, peering up at him through a tangle of hair. "Do you want me to stop?" she asked, and ran her tongue up the length of his rock-hard penis as if it were a great big peppermint stick. "I'll stop if you want me to."

"No, don't stop." He clutched the steering wheel in his fists, struggling manfully to keep his attention on the road while she drove him over the edge with her hot mouth and clever little tongue. "Don't stop."

AND THEN, suddenly, before she was ready for it, the day of the party dawned, bright and hot and sunny, and she realized her Wild West adventure was just about over. Roxanne almost cried, then, as she lay there, staring at the whitewashed ceiling, but the presence of the nurse in the other bed saved her again. She blinked the tears back and got up, determined to enjoy what was going to be her last day with her good-looking dangerous cowboy. One more day—and one more night—that's all she had, all she was going to allow herself.

And she was determined to make it the best night of her life.

And his.

THE PROPOSED PARTY had somehow evolved from a simple welcome home potluck supper with a few close friends into a lavish barbecue that apparently included everyone in the entire county, and the kitchen was a beehive of activity when Roxanne finally made her way downstairs. Jo Beth and her mother, as the official hostesses of the event, were already there, overseeing the food preparation. So was Tom's mother, Molly Steele. Apparently, she had decided to lift her ban on Bowie, except in cases of emergency. Although, in Ms. Steele's mind, anyway, Roxanne was pretty sure she qualified as such. So maybe the ban hadn't been lifted, after all.

The three women were working together in the big, old-fashioned kitchen, a companionable trio with no room for a fourth—especially a fourth with man-killer red nails, questionable morals and possible designs on one of the most eligible bachelors in town.

"Can I do anything to help?" Roxanne asked, even though she already knew what the answer would be. There was no way any of the three women was going to allow her to show off whatever culinary expertise she might possess if Tom Steele was anywhere in the vicinity.

"We've about got it covered in here," Mrs. Jensen

said. "They might need some help out back, though, getting the picnic tables set up and into position."

Which meant, Roxanne knew, that Tom was either in the front yard, doing whatever needed to be done out there or, more likely, down at main corral, seeing that the arrangements for the junior rodeo were progressing apace. Molly Steele and Jo Beth Jensen weren't the only women who were set on bringing Tom into the Jensen family fold.

Roxanne poured herself a cup of coffee, and pushed open the screen door to the back porch. It screeched loudly.

"Someone really ought to put some WD-40 on that," she heard Jo Beth say to the two older women.

She let it the door slam behind her—a petty gesture, but deeply satisfying—and strolled down the steps and across the struggling patch of lawn to where the Padre sat in a rocking chair under a copse of cottonwood trees, his trusty nurse by his side to make sure he didn't overdo, supervising as Jared and Augie set up the barbecue pit.

An entire side of beef—more raw meat than Roxanne had ever seen in one place before—lay on a tarp on top of one of the picnic tables, waiting to be hoisted onto the spit. She tried not to look at it.

"You ever seen a more beautiful side of beef?" asked the Padre as Roxanne approached. "Raised right here on Second Chance."

"Beautiful," she said admiringly, while privately thinking that she might never eat another steak for as long as she lived.

The Padre caught the flicker of distaste in her eyes.

"You're not a vegetarian, are you?" he asked, as if it were a perversion of the worst sort.

"I wasn't," she said dryly.

He laughed and slapped his knee. "A real firecracker," he chortled gleefully.

Roxanne gave in to impulse and bent down to kiss his leathery cheek. "Try not to give your nurse too hard a time today," she said.

He caught her hand as she straightened. "Was that goodbye?"

"No," she said. "That was a deep and abiding appreciation for a good-looking, dangerous man. I'll tell you when it's goodbye."

"Fair enough," he said, and squeezed her hand— just as Molly Steele came out onto the back porch with a pile of bright, checkered tablecloths over her arm.

"Don't you overdo, now, Hector," she called, frowning when she saw the two of them apparently holding hands. "You mind what your nurse says and don't get yourself too excited. And, you—Roxy, isn't it?" She motioned her forward with her free hand. "I'd appreciate it if you would come on over here and help me cover these tables. We can chat a bit while we work and get to know each other."

Roxanne sighed. No way did she want a private tête-á-tête with Tom's disapproving mother. Seeing no way to avoid it, however, she was about to do as she was bid, when she felt the Padre's hand tighten on hers.

"I need Roxy to help me walk down to the barn."

The Padre rose to his feet, using the support of Roxanne's arm for leverage.

"That's what the nurse is here for," Molly said. "And you shouldn't be walking that far, anyway. It's not good for you."

"It is, too, good for me. The doc said walking is the best exercise I could do right now. And I want Roxy to walk with me." He waved the nurse away. "You go help Molly cover those tables. I'll call if I need you."

"Thanks," Roxanne said.

"The thing you got to know about Molly," the Padre said, his head bent companionably to hers as they slowly ambled around the side of the house toward the barn, "is that she means well. She's just become kind of narrow in her opinions and strict in her ways, is all. Comes of her background, I guess, just like it does with most folks. She was kind of wild as a girl, with parents who were too busy to be bothered. She took off with the first cowboy who said he loved her when she was barely fifteen and came home six months later with a full belly and no husband."

"Yes, Tom told me some of the story," Roxanne said, and sipped her coffee.

"She tried to make a go of it on her own but, hell, you know the story...a young unmarried girl, no education, no health coverage, no access to good child care, forced to take one minimum-wage job after another to make ends meet. She pulled herself out of it, though. Admitted she couldn't do it on her own, and did what she had to do to make it right for her boy."

"Tom said she saved him when she gave him to you."

"She did. She saved herself, too. She worked hard, got a college education, and a good job. The thing is, though, instead of being proud of how far she's come, she's ashamed of where she's been. She has no sympathy for the girl she once was, and— Can she see us from where she's at?"

Roxanne glanced back over her shoulder. "No, I don't think so."

"Then let's set a spell, shall we?" He indicated the steps leading up to the porch. "I need to catch my breath."

"Are you all right? Should I call the nurse?"

"No. No, don't call the nurse. I'm fine. Just haven't got my stamina back yet, is all. Now—" he settled down onto the top step, under the shadowed overhang of the porch "—where was I?"

"You said Tom's mom hasn't got any sympathy for the girl she once was."

"No, she hasn't. And she's got no tolerance for anyone else who strays from what she considers the straight-and-narrow, either."

Roxanne looked up at him from where she stood at the foot of the stairs. "And I'm about as far off the straight-and-narrow as a woman can get, is that it?"

"That's certainly what Molly thinks." He gave her a sly, knowing smile from under his bushy gray eyebrows. "I have my doubts about that, though. I'll wager Tom does, too."

Roxanne shrugged. "I wouldn't count on that," she mumbled, and buried her nose in her coffee cup just as Petie came roaring around the side of the house, screaming at the top of his lungs.

"Rooster's here! Rooster's here!" He danced past her, heading down to the barbecue pit under the cottonwoods, then spied the Padre sitting on the steps and made a sharp left turn. "Rooster's here, Padre!" he trumpeted in his piercing little-boy voice, and then changed direction again, heading down toward the barn at a dead run. "Tom! Rooster's here, Tom. Come see. Rooster's here!"

"I swear, that little fella has got more energy than ten bucking bulls," Rooster said to no one in particular as he came around the side of the house. "Plum wears me out to watch him."

He came to a dead stop when he saw Roxanne, a wide smile lighting up his plain, honest face at the sight of her. "Hey, Roxy." He reached out as if to hug her, then stepped back indecisively, a little red around his ears at his presumption.

Roxanne set her empty coffee cup down on the porch step and solved his problem for him by stepping forward and wrapping her arms around his neck. "Hey, pardner." She gave him a good, hard hug. "Congratulations on the big win in Cheyenne," she said, and planted a big, noisy kiss on his cheek.

Rooster blushed to the roots of his hair.

"If you're givin' out your kisses for winnin' rides, I'd just like to say, I beat his score in Wichita *and* Oklahoma City."

Roxanne looked past Rooster's shoulder to the man standing a few feet behind him. "My goodness," she said, her accent as thick and sweet as honey. "Clay Madison. What are you doing here, sugar?"

Rooster gestured toward the young cowboy with a jerk of his thumb. "Clay's my new travelin' partner."

"So," Clay said. "Do I get that kiss?"

Roxy grinned and went into his arms. "That's for Wichita," she said, and kissed him on one cheek. "And that's for Oklahoma City." She kissed him on the other.

It seemed to be her day for kissing cowboys.

Unfortunately, the only one she hadn't kissed yet chose that particular moment to make his appearance.

"You want to unhand that woman," Tom said, "or do I have to rearrange your pretty face for you?"

Clay grinned and tightened his hold on Roxanne, keeping her from stepping away from him. "You're welcome to try," he invited. "Any place. Any time."

"If you don't let go of me, *I'll* rearrange your face for you," Roxanne said, and jabbed him in the gut. She was in too close to do much damage, but it was enough to surprise him into letting her go.

Clay stood there, a half smile on his handsome face, his hand on his abused stomach, watching her as she walked back to the porch and retrieved her coffee cup.

Tom watched Clay watch her, and contemplated the possible satisfaction to be gained in carrying out his threat.

Roxanne sashayed up the porch steps, and sat down on the porch steps next to the Padre to finish her coffee, pointedly ignoring them both. Or pretending to.

"You boys may as well stop pawing at the ground," the Padre said. "She isn't impressed. And we haven't got time for it now, anyway. We've got company comin' up the drive.''

THE PARTY was in full swing by noon. The long gravel driveway was lined with pickup trucks and dusty ranch cars. The kitchen counters were groaning under the platters of fried chicken and baked ham, the fresh corn tamales and enchiladas, the molded gelatin salads and layer cakes and homemade pies that had been brought by the ranchers wives to supplement the side of beef that was slowly roasting to perfection on the spit outside. There was a wild game of tag going on in the backyard and an impromptu horseshoe tournament being waged in the specially constructed horseshoe pits beyond the cottonwood trees. The Padre was sitting on the back porch, where he could keep an eye on the barbecue, playing a fiercely competitive game of checkers with the surgeon who had done his by-pass operation. There were fiddlers on the front porch for those who cared to dance or to just listen. And down in the main corral, out by the barn, the junior rodeo was in full swing under the careful supervision of Tom and Rooster.

Roxanne took it all in, enjoying it to the full, wandering from activity to activity like a child at a county fair, storing up memories in defense against the not-to-distant future when she would be back in her narrow, boring little life in Connecticut. She tossed horseshoes with a jovial white-haired man who turned out to be a county judge, offered unsolicited advice to the checkers players, cheered on the budding rodeo stars, ate more barbecue than she intended to, and danced with anyone who asked.

At the end of the evening, after the fires in the barbecue pit had been carefully banked, and the mothers had gathered up their sleepy children, and the fiddlers had packed up their bows, and the Padre had gone to bed, exhausted after the long day, and Molly Steele had gotten into her little blue Honda and headed back to Dallas, Roxanne found herself right where she wanted to be—alone in the moonlight with Tom.

She leaned back, resting her elbows on the step behind her, and looked up at the stars.

"Tired?" he said.

"Peaceful," she countered, and turned her head to smile at him. "Do you think everybody's actually gone home?"

"I sure as hell hope so. It's coming up on one o'clock."

"And everybody in the house is asleep?"

"It appears that way."

"Then, do you think, if we got a blanket and went out to the barn, we'd be alone?"

He gave her a slow, sweetly wicked smile. "I can guarantee it."

She leaned over and kissed him. "Meet in the tack room in fifteen minutes," she said, and disappeared into the house.

DETERMINED TO SET the scene for romance, Tom used his fifteen minutes to excellent advantage. It only took a few carefully selected props. A bale of hay spread out over the wooden floor for atmosphere, a pair of quilts on top of that for comfort. An electric lantern turned down low to provide the necessary candle glow. A bouquet of sweet peas in a jelly jar to show her that he cared.

"It should be roses," he said when she stepped into the small cozy room, "but we don't have any in the garden."

Roxanne felt the sting of quick, foolish tears and blinked them back, determined not to ruin her last night with him. "Roses would be overkill," she said, and kissed him.

It was soft and sweet and utterly romantic.

"Would you do something for me?" she whispered.

"Anything."

"Would you take off your shirt?"

"Just my shirt?"

"Just your shirt." She smiled. "For now." She slipped her fingers inside the front placket, beneath the pearl snaps. "I'll help you," she said, and gave a little tug, popping them open in one quick motion.

He stripped off the shirt and draped it over one of the saddles on the rack. "Now what?"

"Now you just stand there and let me seduce you."

"You've already done that, Slim. All you have to do is look at me like you're doing right now and I'm putty in your hands."

She arched an eyebrow. "Putty?" she said, and cupped her hand over the fly of his jeans. "It doesn't feel like putty to me."

"Really hard putty," he amended. "Cement." He

pressed his hand to the back of hers, molding her fingers to the solid shape of him. "Concrete."

"I'm going to make you harder. I'm going to make you so hard you hurt." She slid her hand out from under his and backed away. "But no touching."

Tom was already being to ache. "No touching?"

She shook her head. "Not until I tell you. Until I tell you, all you can do is stand there like this—" she took his hands and placed them at his sides, palms flat against his thighs "—and watch." She backed up, well out of reach, and flicked open the top button on her vest. "And want."

He realized then that she'd used her fifteen minutes to change clothes. She was not longer wearing the jeans and tank top she'd had on all afternoon. She'd changed into her ruffled white-eyelet skirt and denim vest.

"Do you remember that night at the Bare Back Saloon, Tom?" She flicked open the second button. "The night when you made me keep my hands against the wall and wouldn't let me touch you?" She worked the third button loose. "Wouldn't let me move until I was nearly crazy with desire?" She lingered on the fourth and final button, playing with it. "Do you remember that night?"

As if he could forget it! "Yes," he said, and licked his lips to ease the dryness.

"Now it's your turn," she said, and slipped the last button from its buttonhole.

The denim parted slightly, revealing a thin slice of flesh between her breasts. She ran her fingertips up and down the opening, those long, red, man-killer nails of hers brushing against her skin, driving him crazy.

"Do you want me to open my vest?"

"Yes."

"Yes, what?"

"Yes…please?"

She smiled in approval and edged the vest open a mere inch, then two, revealing the inner curves of her breasts and the sleek flat line of her stomach.

"More?"

"Yes. Please."

She peeled the two halves of fabric all the way back, slowly, tucking them beneath her arms to display her breasts. And then she cupped her hands over them and began massaging herself, making little circles around her areola, drawing her fingers together to pluck at her own nipples.

"Would you like to touch me like this?"

"Yes, please."

She tilted her head, looking at him from beneath the tangle of her overlong bangs. "No," she said, and smiled when his fingers flexed against his thighs. "Well…" she made a little moue, a suggestion of a pout "…maybe I can come up with something else." She sauntered within reach. "No touching," she warned him, and leaned in, rubbing the very tips of her breasts to his chest. "Do you like that?"

"Yes."

"Tell me."

"I like it very much," he said. "Come closer."

She leaned into him a bit, flattening her breasts against his bare chest.

"Closer," he said.

She shook her head and backed away.

"Have mercy, Slim. You're killing me here."

She tilted her head, considering that. "Sit down," she said. "There." She pointed at a squat wooden stool.

He sat. It put him nearly at eye level with her bare breasts.

"You can't touch them with your hands." She came closer, putting her breasts within reach of his mouth. Barely. "But you can kiss them."

He strained forward, closing his lips around one tempting nipple, and sucked.

Hard.

She moaned and leaned into him, giving him more, turning her body slightly to subtly direct him to the other breast. He took the hint and transferred his attention, giving it the same treatment. She moaned again, and he could feel her shudder. Her hands came up to his head, her fingers raked through his hair.

"Enough!" she said, and jerked his head away.

He nearly howled in frustration.

She stood there for a moment, panting, her breasts quivering with every shuddering breath. Her cheeks were flushed. Her eyes were bright with arousal, and the knowledge of her own seductive powers.

"Would you like to see something else?" she said.

"Yes, please."

She backed away a bit so he would get the full effect, placed her hands on her thighs, and began gathering the fabric of her skirt into her palms. The hem rose, inch by excruciating inch, revealing the tops of

her bright red boots, the lacy white stockings that
sheathed her slender legs, the stocking tops…

"Aw, Slim!" he groaned. "Don't stop now."

"Remember, the last time, when you tore my panties off?"

The skirt rose a half inch higher, revealing a slice
of bare skin above the top of the stockings.

He started to sweat. "Yes. I remember."

"This time you won't have to do that."

"I won't?" he croaked.

The skirt rose another scant inch.

Two.

"Do you know why you won't have to rip my panties off?"

"No," he said, but he could guess.

"Because—" she lifted the skirt to the top of her
pubic mound "—I'm not wearing any."

He came up off the stool in a rush and lunged at
her like a maddened bull.

"No touching," she hollered, but it was too late.

He grabbed her by the waist and spun her around,
bending her over one of the saddles on the rack, and
flipped her skirt up over her head. Holding her there
with a hand on the back of her neck, he used the other
to rip open his jeans and free his erection, then inserted one foot between her booted ankles and swept
it from side-to-side in two quick, convulsive movements, widening her stance. Grasping her hips in his
hands, he stepped forward and thrust into her, burying
himself to the hilt.

She shrieked in mindless ecstasy and pressed back
against him, increasing the pressure. He thrust

once…twice…a third time…and they both came in a blind, cataclysmic explosion of raw passion.

They were both so exhausted, so wrung out by what had just passed between them, that they hung there for a moment or two, both of them bent over the saddle, both of them panting and weak and filled with churning emotions.

Roxanne felt an overwhelming exhilaration, a fierce kind of joy that was almost painful in its intensity. He wouldn't forget her now. No matter what happened, no matter who he married or what his life became, he wouldn't ever forget her.

Tom was swamped with an unnerving, almost brutal tenderness. He'd taken her like an animal, driven to possess her in the most basic, elemental way, and yet there he stood, curled over her body, his overriding instinct to cherish and protect what he had just ravaged.

It wasn't how he had meant for this night to go. He'd planned on romance. He'd planned to shower her with flower petals and kisses. Planned to woo her with soft seductive words, and softer caresses.

He'd planned to tell her how he felt.

But the time to tell a woman you were in love with her wasn't after you'd just mounted her like a stallion in rut and ridden her to exhaustion. Especially when you weren't more than half sure she wouldn't laugh in your face. Falling in love hadn't been part of their bargain, and she hadn't given any indication that she wanted that bargain changed. She had a life up there in Connecticut. A family. Friends. A job. And he knew damned good and well she was used to better than he could give her. She came from cultured, sophisticated people and—despite his fancy college education—he was just a cowboy.

And he really wouldn't want to be anything else.

Not even for her.

The declaration of his feelings would have to wait.

He straightened, lifting her against him with an arm around her waist. She sagged against him, as boneless as a rag doll.

"Are you all right, Slim?"

"I think so." Her voice was soft. Hesitant. Faint. "I'm just so…tired," she managed.

He turned her in his arms and bent slightly, slipping an arm under her knees so he could lift her. Staggering slightly, his own strength curiously lacking, he stumbled to the makeshift bed of hay and quilts, and sank down into the welcoming softness. She lolled against him, already sound asleep. Cuddling her in his arms, he closed his eyes and joined her.

13

ROXANNE WOKE at first light, disturbed by the prickly, uncomfortable feel of straw poking into her bare thigh, and the urgent need to relieve her bladder. She wasn't sure, in that first waking moment, of exactly where she was. And then she became aware of the heat of the body beside her, the weight of his arm over her waist, the soft rush of his warm breath against her shoulder, and it all came flooding back.

Last night.

It had been earthy and magical. Elemental and ethereal. A transcendental experience on a rawly physical plane. And it had made her transformation from good-girl Roxanne to good-time girl Roxy complete.

She'd touched herself like a wanton, tantalizing and teasing her dangerous, good-looking cowboy until he was driven to take her like a beast. And she had reveled in it! There wasn't the slightest sting of embarrassment, not the faintest trace of shame. None of the unspoken taboos and conventions she'd been brought up with had intruded to mar the experience in any way. Her overriding feeling about the night just past was one of supreme satisfaction.

She'd satisfied him.

Utterly.

He'd satisfied her.

Completely.

She'd accomplished what she'd wanted to when she'd set out to seduce him out of his mind. She'd met all her own expectations. Fulfilled every fantasy, except one. And that one hadn't been part of the original bargain. It wasn't fair to change the rules now and ask him to give her something he hadn't bargained for.

It was time for her to go home.

Thankful that he was a heavy sleeper, who always woke slowly, in stages, she picked up his wrist in both hands and gently lifted it off her waist, placing it by his side. Still moving slowly, she sat up and rose to her knees, carefully working her rumpled skirt out from under his thigh. And then she paused and smiled, looking down into his face, wishing, for one fleeting moment, that it had been different. That she had met him under other circumstances, in another place. That she hadn't made the promises she'd made. No muss. No fuss. No strings. And no looking back.

Particularly no looking back!

That was the one she had to remember.

From now on, she would only look forward.

Looking back would hurt too much.

She leaned down and kissed him softly. "Goodbye, sugar," she said.

Rising to her feet, she tiptoed from the tack room.

ROXANNE HAD THE LITTLE attic room to herself. The nurse had gone home after the party last night, her duties at an end, leaving Roxanne free to indulge in a long hot bath and a good hard cry—after which she had to lie down on the bed with a cold washcloth over her eyes for nearly half an hour to soothe the resulting redness away. When she went downstairs, there must be no trace of tears. No evidence of sadness or regret. Good-time girl Roxy had to be completely in charge. It was the only way for good-girl Roxanne to get through the coming goodbyes with her dignity intact.

She did her makeup carefully, using concealer and shadows to camouflage any lingering signs of weepiness, and bright red lipstick to draw attention to the smile she intended to have plastered to her face. Although she tried to linger over the task, she was dressed in a few minutes. Boots and jeans and one of her little sleeveless eyelet blouses didn't lend themselves to a lot of sartorial fusing. Her packing only took another minute or two—she only had the one bag—and before she was really ready, she was heading downstairs to face the music.

Her chin high, her boot heels clicking on the bare wooden treads, she headed for the kitchen as if she were happy to be leaving.

Although there were signs that breakfast had recently been prepared and consumed, the kitchen was empty. Roxanne set her bag on the end of the table and headed for the coffee pot. After pouring herself a cup—and adding the requisite one-half teaspoon of sugar—she plucked the bag off of the table and pushed through the squeaky screened door onto the porch.

It was a beautiful morning, not too hot, yet, although all the signs promised it would be a scorcher.

She could hear cattle bawling somewhere off in the near distance. Chickens pecked around the yard under the cottonwood trees, picking up scraps of food dropped in the grass the night before. Off somewhere near the barn, beyond her field of vision, she heard the boisterous sounds of barking dogs and boys at work and play. A child's laugh—Petie's—drifted out from an upstairs window.

It was paradise, and she had to leave.

The blue Chevy truck—Rooster's ride now that he'd returned the black monster to Tom—was sitting in the yard, the bed already packed with his and Clay's gear. They were headed for the Mesquite rodeo; she planned to ride with them as far as the Dallas-Fort Worth airport. She looked around, wondering where they had gotten to and how long it would be before they were ready to go. She didn't want to drag out her goodbyes. She walked down the wooden stairs, crossed to the truck, and heaved her bag over the side, determined to be ready to leave the minute they were.

The rhythmic squeak of the rocker against the wooden planks of the porch had her turning her head toward the sound. The Padre sat, exactly where he had sat the day before playing checkers with his surgeon, and watched her over his own cup of coffee. She sighed and moved back up the steps and across the width of the porch to his side. Bending down, she kissed him on the cheek.

"That's goodbye," she said.

"I figured it was." He took a sip of his coffee.

"What I didn't figure is that you'd turn out to be such a coward."

"A coward?" she said carefully.

The Padre shook his grizzled head. "I never would have expected it of a firecracker like you."

"Expected what?"

"You running out on him."

She didn't pretend not to know who he was talking about. There was only one *him,* and they both knew it. "I'm not out running out on him. I'm going home. Back to Connecticut were I belong."

"You're running," he said.

"All right, yes, I am. I admit it." Her tone hinted that she was humoring an old man's fancy. "I'm running back home before I get my poor little heart broke," she said, laying on the cornpone accent to show she wasn't serious.

"Have you ever thought that by doing that, you might be breaking his instead?"

"That's impossible."

"Not if he's in love with you."

Roxanne felt her heart leap at the thought. She shook her head. "He's in lust with me," she said. "It's not the same thing."

"No, it's not," the Padre said. "And I'm not saying he doesn't have a healthy case of lust where you're concerned. But he also happens to be in love with you."

Roxanne looked him square in the eyes. "I wasn't joking about how we met," she said. "I picked him up in a bar in Lubbock, just exactly like I told you. I went there *specifically* to pick him up. And then I took him back to my motel room and had sex with him six ways from Sunday before he even knew my name.''

''And your point would be?''

''For crying out loud, Padre! I'm his summer fling. His last hurrah before he retires from the rodeo for good. And he was my walk on the wild side. My study subject for ''What I Did On My Summer Vacation.'' That's all it was ever meant to be between us. That's all it can be.''

''It may have started out that way, but that's not how it ended.'' He gave her a level look. ''For either of you.''

''And your point would be?'' she said, firing his words back at him.

''Don't you think you owe it to him—and your-self—to tell him how you feel? Even if I'm wrong and he isn't in love with you, don't you think you should at least be honest about your *own* feelings?''

''We had an agreement. No muss. No fuss. No strings. When it was over, it was over. And it's over.'' She could feel the hot tears prickling the backs of her eyes. She clenched her hands around her coffee cup and held on, refusing to let them fall. ''I'm not about to change the rules at this stage of the game. It wouldn't be fair to expect more from him now.''

''Not only a coward, but a liar, too.''

''I haven't lied,'' she said, incensed. ''I never lied to Tom.''

''To yourself, Slim,'' the Padre said, using Tom's pet name for her. ''You're lying to yourself.''

She ducked her head, dashing at her cheek with the back of her hand. ''How do you figure that?''

"It's not his feelings you're worried about, it's your own. No, don't go throwing that chin up at me. I'm too old to be taken in by it." He reached out and grabbed her wrist, holding her by his side when she would have turned away. "How's it going to hurt Tom to know you're in love with him? Hmm? If he loves you back, well, that's fine, then, and everybody's happy. If he doesn't, he'll be a mite embarrassed to hear you admit to feelings he doesn't share, but it isn't going to hurt him any. It's your own pride you're worried about. You're so afraid of looking like a fool for falling in love with a man who might not love you, that you're willing to break your own heart over a possibility rather than face the truth of what is."

Roxanne went absolutely still as the reality of the Padre's words sunk in. He was right. It was *her* pride she was worried about. *Her* dignity.

And that was good-girl Roxanne thinking.

She was the one who worried about looking like a fool. She was the one who always pretended to be cool and unconcerned in case anyone thought she cared too much. She was the one who buried everything inside for the sake of good manners and good breeding and not making a messy, emotional scene.

Good-time girl Roxy wasn't anything like that. She believed in letting it all hang out and letting the chips fall where they may. She believed in letting 'er rip, and to hell with worrying about whether her emotions and her needs were dignified or proper.

What good were dignity and pride when your whole future happiness was at stake?

She got a calculating look in her eyes. "Is he still out in the barn?"

"Yep."

"Hold this." She thrust her coffee cup into his free hand, then leaned down and kissed him again, full on the mouth. "That's thank you," she said, and marched on down the stairs and toward the barn with a sassy hip-swinging stride.

"You go get 'em, Roxy," he said, and chortled gleefully.

SHE FOUND HIM in the tack room, right where she'd left him. Or, almost. He'd obviously been up for a while. The quilts they'd slept on were neatly folded on top of the squat little stool. The lantern was back in its accustomed place. The jelly jar of sweet peas was empty and sitting on a shelf next to other jelly jars full of bits and pieces that were used in maintaining and repairing saddles and other tack. He had his shirt on, but it was hanging open over his chest, the collar wet from where he'd either dunked his head in the water trough or held it under a faucet. He was forking up the hay that had been piled on the tack room floor, dumping it into a wheelbarrow by the door.

He barely glanced up as she came into the room. "I thought we said our goodbyes last night," he said without pausing in his work.

"Our goodbyes?"

"That's what you're here for, isn't it? To make it official?"

"Official?" she said, confused by the cold, dispassionate look in his eyes. He'd never looked at her that way before, with no emotion, no feeling.

She began to wonder if the Padre had been wrong.

"Rooster told me you were leaving with him and Clay this morning," he said. "That you arranged it last night. Before you came out here with me."

"Yes," she admitted. "I did."

"So last night was—what? Your final performance? Give the cowboy one last thrill before you packed up and headed out?"

She wanted to lie, wanted to say it wasn't like that at all, but she couldn't. "Something like that," she said. "But the thrill was for my benefit, not yours. I wanted one more memory to take with me."

"Well, you got it."

"Yes, I did."

"So what do you want from me now? Another go-round? One for the road?" He knew he was being a jackass, knew he sounded like a petulant fool, but he'd been ready to declare his love last night. Ready to offer his heart and his hand, and she'd been using him for cheap thrills. It was worse than having her laugh at him. He stabbed another pitchforkful of hay and heaved it toward the wheelbarrow. Some of it fluttered down over the toes of her boots. "I'm afraid I'm too busy right now to accommodate you." He looked her right in the eyes and delivered his killing shot. "Maybe you can get Clay to oblige you."

It took about three seconds for his meaning to sink in. Three seconds in which her fabulous whiskey-colored eyes widened with shock, glistened with hurt, and narrowed in fury.

"That was a really shitty thing to say," she said, fighting to keep the tears out of her voice.

"It was a shitty thing to do."

"What? What did I do? I haven't slept with Clay, and you know it. I haven't ever *wanted* to sleep with Clay. And you know that, too."

"I wasn't talking about Clay. I was talking about last night."

"Last night?" she repeated, at a loss. "Last night was— It was wonderful. It was thrilling. What was so bad about last night?"

"I don't like being used."

"But I wasn't using you. I wouldn't use you. I—" She put her hand on his bare chest, needing the connection.

He stood, quivering beneath her palm like a stallion awaiting the bit, but he didn't move away.

She took encouragement from that. "Do you care for—"

No, that was the wrong way to go about it. It was her feelings she had to be concerned about. Her feelings she had to own up to. She took a deep breath, prepared to make a fool of herself if that's what it took, and plunged in with both feet.

"I love you," she said. "I know it wasn't part of our agreement. I know I promised no strings and no looking back. And I meant it. I still do. If you want me to leave, I'll leave. But I can't go without telling you how I feel. You don't have to do anything about it. You don't have to love me back. I just wanted you to know. I love you. You can take it or leave it, whichever you want. It's up to you."

His eyes heated as he listened to her heartfelt confession. His lips curved. His whole life took a decidedly upward turn, and the world was suddenly bright and shining. He put his hands on her shoulders. "I'll take it," he said, and yanked her against his chest.

Their kiss was long and liquid and leisurely, a silent affirmation of their feelings for each other. She could feel his heart pounding against the palm of her hand, counterpoint to her own wildly beating heart. She smiled up into his eyes as he drew back to look down at her.

"Does that mean you love me, too?" she said, wanting to hear the words.

He bumped his groin against hers. "What do you think, Slim?"

"I think we should skip the preliminaries—" she slipped the toe of her boot behind his ankle and shoved, hard, against his chest, pushing him backward into the mound of hay on the floor "—and get right to it."

He hooked an arm around her knees and brought her down on top of him. "Damn, I like a woman with sass!" he said, and rolled her over, pressing her down into the hay beneath him. His expression sobered as he stared down into her glowing eyes.

"I love you, Slim," he said, giving her the words she needed to hear, the words he needed to say. "I want you for my partner. I want you to share my life and have my babies, and grow old with me. I want you to marry me, Slim. What do you say?"

"I say yes, cowboy."

Epilogue

IT WAS SUNDAY AFTERNOON, the final day of the National Prorodeo finals. Down in the arena, country star Randy Travis had finished singing the national anthem, and the Grand Entry parade was well under way. The state flags of every cowboy in the rodeo were unfurled, carried around the ring by riders mounted on the backs of gleaming palominos. The rodeo queens and their courts rode by, sparkling in sequin-studded Western shirts and elaborately studded jeans, waving and smiling at the stomping and cheering crowd.

Across the strip, in a suite at the Grand Bellagio Hotel and Casino, Roxanne watched the first event on the television screen as she did her hair and makeup, and tried not to listen as the mothers of both the bride and groom bemoaned the tackiness of a Las Vegas wedding. Amazingly, the two women were in perfect accord.

"They could have had a lovely wedding in the front parlor at the Second Chance," Molly Steele said. "The room has an alcove that would have been perfect for a wedding bower. But Tom wouldn't even consider it. He wanted to have the wedding here, in

Las Vegas—'' she said the name as if it were synonymous with Sodom ''—during the rodeo finals.''

"I'd always hoped Roxanne would get married in the garden at our country house. In June, of course, when the roses are in bloom and everything is looking its very best.'' Charlotte Archer sighed at the incomprehensibility of her daughter's choice of locations for her nuptials. "She used to be such a considerate, biddable girl. Never gave her father and me a moment's trouble. And then she turned thirty, and I don't know what happened. I blame it on those awful boots.''

Both women looked toward the offending footwear. The red boots sat, gleaming with fresh polish, at the foot of the bed, an affront to good taste and moderation.

"She wanted a pair when she was nine years old,'' Charlotte confided, "but I refused to buy them for her. I felt bad about it then. I mean, I thought, really, what harm could one pair of boots do? Now we see the results,'' she said, and gestured toward her daughter. "Unbridled excess.''

Roxanne grinned at her mother in the mirror. "Don't you mean *bridaled* excess, Mom?'' she said, and struck a pose, feet primly together, eyes downcast, hands in front of her waist as if she were carrying a bouquet.

She was dressed all in white, as befitting a bride. A white satin corset embroidered with pale-pink rosebuds nipped in her already-slender waist and plumped up her breasts, tiny white bikini panties barely spanned her hips, white lace garters held up gossamer-white silk stockings. Considering the way she was dressed—or rather, undressed—the pose was just the tiniest bit salacious. She planned to strike the same pose for Tom later that night before she let him un-hook her corset.

A knock sounded on the connecting door, causing all three women to jump and look toward it.

"It's me. Tom. You about ready in there?"

Roxanne started for the door, but her mother grabbed her firmly by the arm. "It's bad luck for the groom to see the bride before the ceremony," she warned.

"Especially when she's still in her underwear," Molly said reprovingly as she got up to answer the door. She opened it a crack, so he couldn't peek around the edge and glimpse his bride. "What do you want?" she demanded of her son.

"The bull riding is going to start in less than a hour. We need to get this show on the road if we're going to get it done before then. Everything's ready in here. All we need is the bride."

"Roxanne is just putting her dress on now. She'll be out in a minute," Molly said, and started to shut the door.

Tom put his hand on it, stopping her. "Wait a min-ute, Mom," he said, suddenly looking as nervous as a schoolboy. "Give this to her for me, will you?" He slipped a flat jeweler's box through the crack. "And tell her I love her with all my heart."

"She heard you," Molly said dryly, but she was smiling when she turned away from the door and car-ried the box to her soon-to-be daughter-in-law.

Roxanne accepted it with trembling fingers. He'd

already given her an engagement ring. It sparkled on the ring finger of her left hand, an antique square cut ruby that matched her ruby-red nail polish. She hadn't expected anything else. The box contained a necklace in the same gleaming silver metal as the setting for her ring. It was as delicately wrought as cobweb, the chain nearly invisible, with a tiny number seven suspended from it. Her eyes clouded up with emotion. Seven had been the number on the door of her motel room that first night in Lubbock.

"Lucky number seven," she murmured, remembering the way he had carried her to the room that night. And what had happened after.

"Don't get all blubbery now," her mother said. "We haven't got time for you to redo your makeup." She took the necklace from Roxanne's fingers and fastened it around her neck. The tiny number seven nestled in the soft hollow at the base of her throat, in the spot that Tom liked to kiss when he was feeling especially tender and romantic.

"Be careful now," Molly said, as they maneuvered the dress over her head. "Try not to mess up your hair."

"As if you could tell with that mop," Charlotte said, but she was smiling.

Unlike the risqué underwear, the dress was elegant and demurely ladylike. Made of matte satin with a dull sheen, it had a simple sweetheart neckline that merely hinted at the presence of cleavage. The illusion sleeves were long and narrow, ending in a flat satin cuff at her wrists. The skirt flared slightly from the natural waist, ending a few inches above her ankles to show off the red cowboy boots she intended to wear with it.

Both of the mothers sighed when Roxanne stomped into them, but neither one of them said anything. Roxanne was as adamant about the boots as she had been about the location.

They helped her fasten on her veil and handed her the bouquet—sweet peas and baby's breath—and suddenly, she was ready. There was no more to do, no more preparations to make.

Molly opened the door into the main room of the suite, signaling Roxanne's father. There was a rustling and a bit of chatter, and then everyone was settled in their places, congregating on either side of the room to leave a path for the bride. The organist began to play softly, signaling the bride's entrance. Roxanne took a deep breath, slipped her hand into the crook of her father's elbow, and stepped into the flower-bedecked living room of the suite.

Her eyes found Tom's immediately and she focused on him, her gaze never wavering as she made her way through the throng of people crowded into the room. All the Second Chance boys were in attendance, from Petie on up to Jared and Augie. Rooster and his new traveling partner and fellow bull riding finalist Clay were there, decked out in their fanciest rodeo shirts. The Padre waited beside Tom, ready to offer his support as best man and maid of honor combined.

Tom held his hand out as she approached. She let go of her father's arm and reached out, laying her fingers in his. He brought them to his lips for a brief butterfly kiss and then, together, as one, they turned to the justice of the peace.

"Everyone please remove your hats," he intoned severely, and then, when everyone had done as he requested, "Dearly beloved," he began.

Five minutes later, the new Mr. and Mrs. Steele were gazing at each other, dewy eyed with love, identical smiles of blissful delight on their faces.

Forty minutes later, they were at the rodeo finals—still in their wedding finery—watching Rooster ride to the winning score on the back of the Widow Maker. Rooster stood in the center of the arena as the announcer broadcast his name and score over the loudspeaker, a wide grin on his face, his arms raised overhead in triumph. Roxanne gave a loud, raucous, unladylike whoop of joy and tossed her bridal bouquet into the ring in tribute.

And then she tossed herself into her husband's waiting arms.

The Cities
New York, Houston, Seattle

The Singles
Dating dropouts
Chelsea Brockway, Gwen Kempner, Kate Talavera

The Solution—THE SKIRT!

Can a skirt really act as a man magnet? These three
hopeful heroines are dying to find out! But once
they do, how will they know if the men of their
dreams really want *them*...or if the guys are just
making love under the influence?

Find out in...

Temptation #860—*MOONSTRUCK IN MANHATTAN*
by Cara Summers, December 2001

Temptation #864—*TEMPTED IN TEXAS*
by Heather MacAllister, January 2002

Temptation #868—*SEDUCED IN SEATTLE*
by Kristin Gabriel, February 2002

It's a dating wasteland out there!

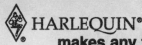

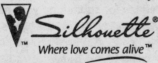